HANG THE SHERIFF HIGH

When the sheriff of Serenity, Bill Mitchell, is convicted of robbery and murder, men flock to see him executed. Then a newspaperman arrives, named William Palmer. Supposedly looking for a story, Palmer has reasons to wish Mitchell dead . . . Searching for the truth, he joins in a bid to snatch the sheriff from the gallows. When the range war Mitchell had been holding at bay erupts into life, Palmer risks death and the loss of his new love in a race to bring peace and justice back to Serenity.

EUGENE CLIFTON

HANG THE SHERIFF HIGH

Complete and Unabridged

LINFORD
Leicester

First published in Great Britain in 2005 by
Robert Hale Limited
London

First Linford Edition
published 2006
by arrangement with
Robert Hale Limited
London

British Library CIP Data

Clifton, Eugene
    Hang the sheriff high.—Large print ed.—
Linford western library
    1. Western stories
    2. Large type books
    I. Title
    823.9'2 [F]

    ISBN 1–84617–202–0

Published by
F. A. Thorpe (Publishing)
Anstey, Leicestershire

Set by Words & Graphics Ltd.
Anstey, Leicestershire
Printed and bound in Great Britain by
T. J. International Ltd., Padstow, Cornwall

This book is printed on acid-free paper

1

In all his seventeen years Jake Jefferson had never turned down the chance of a fight, but he'd overstretched himself this time. The man with the wall-eye was ten years older and twice his weight, and he fought dirty. He recoiled as Jake's knuckles connected, but he came back hunching over a right hook to the ribs, masking his left hand as it dropped to jab hard below the belt. Jake's face paled between the reddening bruises the encounter had already earned him and he ducked away, only to find Rollo Corder moving in to slam a meaty fist at his head.

Little Pete stood up against the barn under the HUCKLE & MILLER DRY-GOODS sign. His forehead creased as Jake staggered. He had one enormous hand round the neck of Rollo's brother Thaddeus, immobilizing

1

him, and Rufus, the youngest of the Corder brood, was tucked under his other arm. Like his father, Little Pete didn't hold with fighting, in part because he rarely found an opponent anywhere near big enough for a fair contest, but he had no objection to evening up the odds a little for his friends. His face cleared as he shouted a greeting to the square chunky figure who'd appeared in the entrance to the alleyway.

'Billy!'

'The newcomer came running with an enthusiastic whoop, and the two younger Corder brothers squirmed and wriggled in Little Pete's grasp. Billy waded into the swirl of dust rising around Jake and his two opponents, unseen by Rollo who was hovering close to the wall-eyed man. Seeing an opening he swung another vicious blow at Jake's undefended head but it never landed. Billy's fist met Rollo's stubbly chin with an arm-numbing jolt. It was a lucky shot, Rollo went down and his head made violent contact with the wall of the barn. He grunted and lay still.

Before Billy could reach him Jake was down too, retching and choking with the wall-eyed man's boot slamming into his gut. With a roar of rage Billy flung himself at Wall-eye, overwhelming him with a torrent of punches to face and chest, driving him backwards until he tripped over the unconscious Rollo's legs to fall sprawling in the dirt.

With Little Pete's attention on Billy, Thaddeus Corder chose that moment to break free, slamming his clenched fists into the huge youth's ribs and wrenching away from his grasp. He tackled Billy round the waist and brought him down. They landed in a tangle of arms and legs and rolled across the alleyway exchanging a flurry of blows; they were old enemies, both eager to renew hostilities. Billy laughed as his fist thudded into Thaddeus's nose with a satisfying crunch, a spray of blood deluging them both, but then a powerful right from Thaddeus's bony knuckles drove all the breath from his lungs and for a moment the sunlight faded to grey. Feeling Billy recoil Thaddeus stopped punching and tried for a lock on his neck. Billy had just enough sense left to squirm away, shunting himself along on his back to keep out of reach of the long, questing fingers.

A hand grabbed Billy by the collar and jerked him upright, making him gag. He shook his addled head and rounded on this new attacker, blinking fast in an attempt to clear his vision. He froze. A wide-brimmed hat shaded Bill Mitchell's face, but it didn't hide the flint-grey eyes, filled with a cold, hard anger.

'That's enough.'

Billy wondered for the thousandth time how the sheriff moved so quick and so quiet; it was like he had a sixth sense for trouble, especially where Billy and his friends were concerned. Mitchell tossed him painfully against the wall. For Billy the savage joy of the fight was instantly replaced by a cold and bitter fury.

Wall-eye pushed himself up from the ground and turned to run. 'Stay right there.'

The man skidded to a standstill, taking in the sheriff's stance, the broad shoulders relaxed, feet a little apart, thumbs hitched into his belt so his right hand hung poised and easy above the Colt Peacemaker in its worn holster. Watchful grey eyes bored into him from beneath the broad-brimmed hat. Billy saw thoughts fleet swiftly across Wall-eye's face, reading the moment when he decided he was beat, a second before he lifted his hands in a gesture of submission. Bill Mitchell lifted Wall-eye's .45 from its holster and pushed him back beside Billy and Little Pete. Jake Jefferson staggered to his feet and limped across to join them.

The sheriff walked along the ragged line of antagonists. Jake looked up at the man behind the badge with the trace of an impudent grin and dark eyes dancing, though blood was running freely down his battered face. Bill Mitchell met his look briefly and grunted.

Little Pete stood head and shoulders above the rest, but he kept his eyes on the ground. The sheriff sighed.

'Little Pete, get on home to your pa, I ain't wasting my time telling you to stop hanging around with these log-heads. Same goes for you,' Mitchell added, jerking his head at Thaddeus Corder. 'Take the kid and get out of town.'

'I didn't do nothin',' Rufus shot back, his voice switching from growl to squeak on the last word. He flushed as Jake laughed and his muscles bunched, but his brother grabbed him by the arm.

'What about Rollo?' Thaddeus's voice came thick through the blood streaming from his broken nose.

'He'll be along,' the sheriff replied. 'Now git.'

The alleyway seemed suddenly quiet as the dust drifted slowly back to the ground. Rollo Corder stirred and grunted, lifting his head out of the dirt. Mitchell glanced at him, then moved on, coming face to face with Billy.

They were of a height, and despite his lack of years Billy was already almost as broad in the shoulders as the man facing him; he met the sheriff's glare with one of equal intensity, his square jaw set, grey eyes cold as a midwinter sky.

'I'm really sorry, Sheriff,' Jake said, taking a half-step as if to come between them, 'but this bum was badmouthing the Lazy T, and I guess I lost my temper. Billy didn't take no part in it, not until Rollo joined in.' He stirred the rising figure at their feet with his toe. 'C'mon fatso, you ain't hurt. Never been a Corder born that wasn't solid wood from the neck up.'

Rollo growled and got to his knees.

'You let them push you into a fight,'

Bill Mitchell said heavily. 'Again.'

'You can't expect him to take — ' Billy began.

'Shut up!' With barely suppressed fury Mitchell ground out the words. 'You,' he pointed at Wall-eye, 'help young Corder up. The four of you can cool your heads in jail for a while.'

As Wall-eye turned and bent down to obey Rollo pushed him aside.

'I ain't goin' nowhere with that young punk,' he said. 'I've had enough of them Jeffersons thinkin' they own this territory.' He came upright and grabbed his black-handled .38 from its holster, small eyes focusing on Jake Jefferson, hard with hatred.

The crash of a shot echoed around the alleyway. Wall-eye stared in disbelief as Rollo jerked away from him, blood spurting from his right shoulder. Rollo's gun thudded to the ground.

The sheriff didn't appear to have moved, but the Peacemaker was in his hand, its long barrel smoking.

'You ready to step across to the

jail now, Corder, or you want to argue some more?'

Rollo stood white-faced and grimacing with pain, his left hand clutching at his arm just below his shattered shoulder. He glared at Jake and spoke through clenched teeth.

'You wait, Jefferson. You won't always have your pa's tame lawman watchin' over you.'

Bill Mitchell waited for him to walk by.

'Jake, pick up that gun and bring it here.' The youngster obeyed and the sheriff thrust the .38 into his belt. 'Now move, all of you.'

'You sure know how to pick a fight,' Billy muttered sourly to his friend as they crossed the street.

'Yeah,' Jake replied, licking blood from his lip with a grin, 'But it took the sheriff to finish it. Did you see that draw? Fast as greased lightning.'

★ ★ ★

A narrow corridor led from the rear of the sheriff's office to the jailhouse, a stone-built block with four narrow slit windows in the back, admitting a mean ration of light and hardly wide enough to let a rat through. Not that there was much to look at, only a solitary barn, then a hundred miles of Colorado prairie. Billy and Jake sat side by side on a wooden bunk, their backs to the window, looking down the corridor where the office door stood open.

Jake was still ashen-pale, holding on to his aching belly, but Billy's face was flushed with anger.

'He's got no right holding us in here,' he said. 'We supposed to run and hide when the Corders come into town?'

'You figure we can argue with him?' Jake tilted his head towards the office, dropped his hand to his belt and pretended to pull a gun from an imaginary holster. 'Serenity ain't big enough for the three of us. Git out of town and don't bother to come back,' he mimicked, sounding so much like the sheriff that Billy laughed despite his fury.

Rollo Corder shared the other cell with the wall-eyed man. He lay on the bunk with his face nearly as white as the bandage swathing his shoulder; there were beads of sweat on his forehead and his mouth was drawn into a tight line. Since the doctor had left he hadn't said a word; before that his range of obscenities had added comprehensively to Billy and Jake's education.

A voice from the office jerked Billy's attention back to the corridor.

'What about the boys?' It was Deputy Nat Grimes, and as he spoke he moved across the office so Billy could see the back of his grey head through the open doorway.

'What about 'em?' the sheriff responded tautly. 'All right, fetch Jake out here, I'll try talking to him before Quentin arrives. The other one can sit in there and rot for all I care.'

Nat Grimes came to unlock the door, giving Billy a swift wink and leaving the

11

door open behind him.

'Turn that key in the lock,' Bill Mitchell shouted. 'This is supposed to be a jail.'

With a smile that etched deeper lines on his wrinkled face the deputy noisily locked the cell door while it was still ajar.

'Seems me an' Rollo ain't the only ones around here who's unpopular,' Wall-eye said. 'That sheriff sure don't like you, kid. What you do to upset him?'

'Got myself born,' Billy replied shortly. 'He's my father.'

2

Rollo began to snore softly. Wall-eye peered through the bars at Billy, his eye shining like a pale lamp in the dim light.

'What's between you and the Corders?' he asked abruptly. 'I joined Red Corder's outfit two weeks ago, soon learned how he feels about the Jeffersons, but nobody said nothin' 'bout the sheriff's son.'

'You just said it,' Billy replied. 'Jake Jefferson's my friend.'

'But the sheriff ain't.' The man's mouth twisted in a humourless smile. He took the makings of a cigarette from his vest pocket. 'First man I ever killed was the bastard who sired me. Tell you what, boy, you get hold of the key from that friendly deputy an' I'll deal with your pappy for you. Reckon that'd please my boss too, I doubt if this boy of his'll ever sling lead right-handed again. How 'bout it?'

For a long moment there was no sound but Rollo's noisy breathing, then slowly Billy shook his head.

'No.'

'But it's temptin' ain't it.' The man with the wall-eye struck a match against the stone wall of the cell and laughed.

Billy turned away, walked quietly out through the open cell door and along the passage to listen outside the office.

'Won't you ever learn?' His father sounded dispirited and Billy grinned, picturing Jake standing in front of him, bruised and bloody and unrepentant. The outer door of the office was flung open, then slammed shut so hard it rattled every window in the building.

Quentin Jefferson had a powerful voice, even when he wasn't aggravated.

'What's he done this time, Bill? I swear, if I'd known how much trouble this pup was going to be I'd have drowned him at birth.'

With growing fury Billy heard his

14

father's version of the fight. How come he always got the blame? Deaf after a while to the familiar tally of his faults, Billy clenched his fists, listening to the blood thundering in his head. Maybe Wall-eye had the right idea.

By the time Billy got his temper buttoned down again Quentin Jefferson was talking.

'Send him to the Lazy T. I swear neither one of them will come into town for the next six months. I'll work 'em so hard they won't have the strength to get into any more trouble.'

'You do what you like with your own,' Bill Mitchell replied, 'but I'm not asking you to take mine. You tried last summer and look where it got you. Reckon you must still be missing that prize bull.'

Billy scowled. It was Jake who'd shot the bull, not him, though admittedly he'd done it to stop Billy getting himself killed. There were times Billy almost wished he hadn't bothered.

His father hadn't finished.

'He'll never make much of a cowboy and you know it. Any more than he'll make a bank clerk or a storekeeper or a goldarned mule-driver!'

'That's not — ' Jake began. Billy winced at the slap of flesh against flesh. 'No lip from you,' Quentin Jefferson growled. 'Reckon I've been too soft, boy, time you learnt to show some respect.' There was a creak as the rancher stood up out of his chair. 'So long, Bill, and thanks for not pressing charges. If you change your mind about that young 'un of yours you know where to send him.'

As the outer door slammed again Billy returned to the cell and threw himself on to the bunk. A minute later Nat appeared, jangling the keys in his hand and making a show of finding the right one.

Bill Mitchell waited in the passage, watching the old man release his son. They came face to face in the doorway. Billy's mouth was set hard, tension drawing fine lines between his brows, his grey eyes glittering as he stared at the stubborn square-jawed man glowering back at him. Nat Grimes guffawed and the sheriff turned on him with a snarl.

'You find something funny?'

The deputy shook his head.

'Two twigs off the same branch, that's all,' he replied, dousing his grin.

The street door opened again and a skinny pale-faced man of about twenty-five looked in.

'Sh . . . Sheriff? R-Red C-C-Corder just w-went into the G-G-Golden G-Gate. L-looks like he heard about the f-fight.'

'Thanks, Ethan. I'd best talk to him.' He glared at Billy. 'Go home. We'll talk when I get back.'

* ★ *

Hester Mitchell stood up quickly. 'Why don't you and your friends take the air on the veranda, Kate,' she said.

'Why don't you just say you want us

out of the way while you talk to Billy,' Kate replied pertly, with a scathing look at her brother.

'That's enough from you, young lady.' Their mother gave her a push. Kate pouted but turned to leave. Daisy Salmon was already on her way, glancing up as she passed Billy, fair curls bobbing and cheeks dimpling. Used to Daisy, Billy hardly noticed. He was looking at the other girl; he didn't recall seeing her before. Her hair was dark but shot with gleaming red copper, and though she kept her face turned away he got a tantalizing glimpse of smooth, pale skin and a generous mouth. For a moment he almost forgot the fury bubbling through his veins.

'You'd better tell me what happened this time,' Hester said, when the three girls had gone and the door was closed behind them.

'There's no point talking,' Billy said, slumping into a chair. 'I'm leaving, Mom.'

She didn't argue, sitting down across the table from him as if she was suddenly weary.

'Where will you go?' she asked. 'Not to the Lazy T?'

'No. I'm heading East. I'll take the train.' The railroad hadn't yet made it to Serenity, though there were rumours that surveyors had been seen between there and Pacetown, the nearest place with a rail depot.

'You'll need money.'

He looked at her uneasily; he had exactly two dollars and nineteen cents. He'd planned to hide himself in a freight wagon, though the guards were said to be tough on hobos; could be he'd find himself thrown off the train in the middle of noplace. Hester sighed and stood up, going into the pantry. She came back a minute later carrying a small wooden box.

'I knew this day would come. Your father's stubborn streak runs through you like a stain. It's been three years since I heard either one of you say a kind word to the other.' She took a wad of bank-notes from the box and silenced his protests with a wave of her hand. 'It's all right, this money's my own, I sold some of my mother's things a while ago. It's only fair, Kate will get her jewellery.' Her eyes were swimming with tears. 'I won't waste time trying to change your mind. You're grown now; do what you want,' she said, 'only . . . ' She faltered.

'Stay out of trouble,' he finished flatly. 'You're no better than him, Mom, so sure I'll turn out bad.'

'That wasn't what I was going to say,' she retorted, dashing a hand at her damp cheeks and straightening her back. 'Just that I'd appreciate a letter now and then, so I know where you are and how you're getting along. If you want to leave before your father gets home you'd best hurry. How will you get to Pacetown?'

'Jake'll lend me a horse. I can walk to the Lazy T.'

'There's no need for that. You can

take Blackie. Ask Quentin to have one of the hands bring her back tomorrow.'

Billy was momentarily silenced. His mother loved the little mare her husband had given her; she never let anyone else ride Blackie. He pushed back his chair and leant over to kiss her.

'Go and pack,' Hester said. 'I'll put up some food for you. Unless I'm mistaken you've had nothing since breakfast.'

He nearly made it. Blackie was saddled and tied up outside, and Billy was just picking up his mother's old carpet-bag when his father appeared at the door. Bill Mitchell looked from his wife to Billy and back.

'You going out, Hester?'

She flushed. 'No. Billy's borrowing Blackie. I said he could.'

'Not till he and I have had a talk.' His daughter sat with her friends at the table, looking half-scared, half-amused. 'Kate, it's time your friends went home. You can walk them down the street.'

This time the dark girl glanced back,

raising her head just long enough for Billy to see large eyes that could have been blue or green; it was like looking into pools of deep still water. The evening felt suddenly hot, as if there was a storm coming. There was no time to wonder at the sudden change, for in an instant she was gone and he had other things on his mind.

'Hester . . . ' The sheriff stood holding the door open, looking at his wife.

'I'm staying right here, Bill,' she said quietly. 'Whatever you and Billy have to say to each other I intend to hear.'

As always when his mother put her foot down Billy was amazed to see his father give in; he simply nodded and closed the door, stepping to the other side of the table and looking at Billy across it.

'I hardly know how to start,' Bill Mitchell began heavily. 'You've dragged my name through the mud one time too many. I'm tired of wasting my breath talking to you and I'm sick of apologizing for you. It ain't fair to Quentin but I can't see any other way. Get yourself out to the Lazy T right now and don't show your face in this town until you've learnt to act civilized. And if you cause trouble for the Jeffersons like last time I'll have the hide off your back.'

'I'm through listening to you,' Billy said, his fists clenching. 'I'm not going to the Lazy T, that's about the only thing we agree on: I'd make a pretty poor cowboy. I ain't staying here no more. Just because my father's the county sheriff I'm scarce allowed to breathe but I'm out of line. I don't do no worse than Little Pete or Jake.'

'Little Pete's a boy to be proud of,' Bill Mitchell roared, losing his fragile grasp on his temper. 'He'll be a damned fine blacksmith like his pa. And for all his size he's a peaceable soul, 'cept when he's tagging around with you. As for Jake, the way Quentin spoils him it ain't surprising he acts wild now and then, but he works hard and he's got a sensible head on his shoulders. He'll take good care of the Lazy T when it's his turn.'

'Same old thing!' Billy spat out the words, his face a mirror of his father's. 'You're mad at me because I'm not like you. You can't understand why I don't want to wear a tin star on my chest and strut around town so folk can admire me.'

'You young whippersnapper!' The sheriff leant across the table so their faces were only inches apart, his breath hot on his son's cheek. 'You think I care what you do? If you ever showed any inclination to work I'd be happy. You never stuck at nothing in your life.'

'I had a job last year, till you sent me off to work at the Lazy T.'

'You call that a job, sweeping out the store and loading wagons a couple of hours a day? Even Ethan Jones does better for himself than that.' Bill Mitchell raised a clenched fist, pushing Hester aside when she caught hold of it. 'I swear if it didn't mean I'd have to see you every single moment of the day I'd slap you back in that jail and throw away the key.'

'You can't lock him up just because he doesn't do as he's told.' Hester's voice was sharp. 'The boy's nearly seventeen.'

The sheriff's mouth was twisted, his breath coming quick and noisy.

'Yes, you're right. He's old enough to take responsibility for his behaviour. I could bring charges for the last dozen times he's committed a breach of the peace. Maybe the judge would have him sent to the state penitentiary. They'd settle him down some there!'

'Bill!' Hester's shocked voice brought her husband's head whirling round to look at her but he was unrepentant, his face set.

'Goldarnit, Hester, I don't know how I'll ever repay Quentin for taking him on again after what happened last time, but if that boy don't get out of this house right now I swear I'll not answer for my actions.'

'Don't worry, I'm going,' Billy snarled. He pushed the table so hard it knocked his father to the floor. He laughed harshly. 'Big man! If I never see you again it'll be too soon.'

'Billy!' Hester grabbed her son's arm. He pulled away and dragged the door open. Ripping Blackie's rein free he flung himself into the saddle and drummed his heels into the little mare's sides.

Bill Mitchell thrust up from the floor, taking hold of his wife when she would have blocked his way and lifting her aside.

'Bill!' Hester called. 'Let him go. Please!'

'Not this time,' he ground out. She followed him into the street but he was already in the saddle, his big bay springing away in pursuit of the mare.

3

Serenity hardly noticed the arrival of the midday train. The town had grown used to the urgent clang of the bell and the hiss of steam as the iron horse rode in, and today folk had other things on their minds. The dusty roadways were full of horses and wagons with a mix of townsmen, cowboys and drifters competing for space on the side-walks. A visitor might have thought he'd happened on a local festival, except that the women were mostly staying behind doors.

Upwards of twenty men left the passenger car to add to the crowds. One of them, an Easterner in a brown city suit and derby hat strode fast up Main Street. He'd left the depot well behind before he attracted attention.

'Hey, look at the dude.' The shout came from a group of cowboys idling outside the Ace of Spades saloon. One stepped forward, a man in his thirties with a face tanned to the colour of old leather, a battered Stetson tipped well back on his head. 'I sure like that hat. Hey, mister, lemme buy you a drink.' The Easterner paid no attention, and when the cowboy leapt into his path he merely side-stepped.

'C'mon stranger, that ain't civil. I was talkin' to you.' The cowboy pursued him, accompanied by a group of grinning onlookers. 'You gotta learn Western manners.'

'You tell him, Buck,' one of his followers shouted. 'He ain't bein' po-lite.'

The stranger angled across the street but the cowboy ran to get ahead of him again, forcing him to stop. There was a pause just long enough to take a breath, the man they called Buck narrowing his eyes at what he saw. The face beneath the derby hat had two unmatched halves; the right side was smooth, almost boyish, belonging to a young man who'd seen maybe twenty-five years, but the left was marred by a terrible puckered scar running from beside the eye to the corner of the mouth, where it pulled the lip up into a permanent sardonic smile. Looked at from that side the stranger was as old as the devil himself. Pasting a grin back on his face, Buck pointed at the derby.

'I'd sure like to try that hat for size.'

The stranger returned his gaze, grey eyes taking the cowboy's measure.

'If you're looking for a fight I'd be happy to oblige at some later time, but just now I'm in rather a hurry,' he said.

There were laughs and catcalls at this, and several voices could be heard mimicking his Eastern accent. 'Hey dude, you gonna *oblige* me when you're done with Buck?'

'He's in *rayther* a hurry. Come on, Buck, show the man some Western hospitality.'

Buck laughed and bounced on his toes, making a show of limbering up. With an audible sigh the stranger looked to one side and then the other before dropping the bag he carried. Lightning-fast his right fist came up and caught Buck in the ribs. As the cowboy's head jerked forward and his mouth dropped open the heel of the stranger's left hand struck him on the chin, bringing Buck's teeth together with a snap and sending him arcing back to stretch his length on the street. The encounter was so brief and unexpected that the stranger had picked up his bag and walked half a block before anyone thought of following him. Buck sat up slowly, feeling his jaw.

There was an armed man standing guard outside the sheriff's office, and those cowboys who'd tagged along behind the stranger fell back and watched as the dude stepped up and spoke to him. The deputy gave a nod and vanished inside.

The Easterner stood at the end of the sidewalk and looked west. There was a barn standing well back from the rear of the jailhouse. On either side of it a mix of shacks and cabins strung out to form a wide, untidy thoroughfare; compared to Main Street it was quiet, it didn't look like the cheap cantina or the barber's shop were doing much trade.

There was an obvious new addition to the view, stark-cut timber rearing against the sky. A man wearing a deputy's badge leant against the foot of the scaffold, tossing a coin into the air and catching it, over and over, studying the result of each gamble. Heads or tails. Life or death. The stranger watched him a full minute before he turned back, his old young face unreadable.

Several hands reached to pull Buck to his feet. Another cowboy, a thin-faced man with an untidy moustache, came walking fast from the direction of the rail depot.

'What was that all about, Buck? Boss wasn't on the train, but McDonald says he might get a ride on the freight, be through about six.'

'OK Joe,' Buck said, 'ain't worth goin' back to the ranch. Anybody got the price of a bottle of whiskey?'

'You reckon that dude's the hangman?' Joe hazarded.

'With a punch like that?' Buck said, slapping his dusty hat against his knee then putting it back on his head. He probed in his mouth and discovered a loose tooth. 'He don't need a rope.'

'Yeah, but if he was, I reckon the boss'd want to know. Wasn't nobody else got off the train who looked likely.'

'You wanna go ask him?' Buck asked.

'Man can't get hanged if there's no hangman,' another of the cowboys said, glancing again at the dude outside the sheriff's office.

Two men left the Golden Gate saloon and came sauntering across the street, one of them young and stringy with a mop of thick red hair, the other an older man with a wall-eye and an unhealthy yellowish tinge to his skin.

'Thought the dude in the fancy hat was visitin' your boss,' the redhead said, coming to a halt in front of Buck. 'Guess I was wrong; seems he shares my opinion of the Jeffersons' outfit.' His mouth twisted into an unpleasant smile. 'Always said you was soft, Buck, can't even lick a dude.'

The mood in the street had changed in a heartbeat, a malevolent undercurrent running between the two men. The grin with which Buck had encountered the stranger was gone, replaced by a hard-eyed glare.

'Shut your mouth, Corder, or I'll shut it for you.'

'Sure, that's the Lazy T's idea of a fair fight, two against a half-dozen,' the youngster jeered. 'I'll take you on any time, Buck, when you ain't got that rabble backin' you. Bet you ain't willin' today, not when your boss lost his pet lawman.'

There was a growl of anger from the cowhands behind Buck. He glanced around.

'Like the dude said, I'll be happy to oblige. Keep out of it,' he added, handing his hat to Joe and unbuckling his gun belt. 'Rufe's had this comin' for long enough.'

The red-haired youngster tossed his own belt to the wall-eyed man.

'You heard him, Whitey, this is just the two of us.'

They circled warily for a moment, then Buck waded in, landing a solid blow on the redhead's ribs in exchange for a crunching punch to his head. After that there was no more playing for position. The redhead came in low, grappling Buck to the ground, his thumbs seeking the cowboy's eye sockets, but Buck rolled, taking the younger man with him so he had the advantage of his greater weight, doing some damage with knee and boot before they separated and came upright again.

Despite the redhead's youth they were evenly matched. He had a longer reach, and he was fast on his feet, and for a while they traded blows, lurching between the onlookers who cheered them on; it was anybody's fight. But Buck was older and tougher, his weather-beaten face and prairie-hardened body soaking up the punishment. Blood ran from his nose and mouth as he took what the redhead doled out and came back for more, eventually delivering a jolting blow to the head followed by a smash to the beardless jaw that sent his opponent flying.

Yelling encouragement the crowd surged up and down the street while the fight ebbed and flowed. As it approached the sheriff's office the Easterner stepped down off the sidewalk, pushing through the cheering mob to see the end. Buck didn't follow up his advantage. He stood taking a breather, content to let his opponent come back to him. The redhead staggered to his feet, his bright hair matted with blood from cuts on his ear and forehead. He paused for a moment, his hands at his belt, his body almost doubled over; he looked to be finished, reeling towards Buck with his head down.

The flash of sunlight on steel was there and gone in a second.

'Look out, Buck!' The stranger shouted the warning as the younger man came rushing in, his hand jabbing up towards Buck's belly. The cowboy slid aside just in time and the blade sliced across his forearm instead of plunging into his body.

Buck let out a roar of rage and felled his opponent with a mighty smash from his right. He stepped forward, massaging his knuckles, one foot stamping down on the fingers that wielded the knife, but the weapon had already fallen from the youngster's nerveless hand.

With a puzzled look on his face Buck scanned his audience, trying to see the man who'd shouted to him.

'Where'd the dude go?' he asked, swiping blood and spittle from his chin.

★　★　★

The stranger removed the Derby hat from his head, nodded at the man behind the sheriff's desk and handed him a small piece of pasteboard.

'I'm William Palmer,' he said, 'from the *Eastern Gazette*.'

'Sheriff Slim Ketteridge.' The lawman looked the newcomer up and down, frowning slightly. The scar took his attention first; it was impossible to miss, but there was more to the man than a spoiled face. The dude looked to be in his mid twenties, not tall but with power in the broad chest and shoulders under the fancy suit. He carried no spare flesh, and he stood square, light on his feet like a fighter. The grey eyes met his steadily, a few faint lines running up from between the brows and disappearing under straight brown hair.

Having finished his scrutiny Ketteridge turned to the big pot-bellied man who'd summoned Palmer into the office.

'What's goin' on out there, Mike?'

'Just Rufe Corder an' Buck lettin' off a little steam. Don't look like anyone else got involved. You want I should bring 'em in?'

'We got enough to do, don't want them cluttering up the cells. Keep an eye on things, make sure the crowd breaks up peaceable.' The sheriff turned his attention back to the Easterner. 'Have I seen you before someplace?' he asked.

'I doubt it. People don't tend to forget a face like mine. I'm here to write about the Mitchell case, Sheriff. If there's one thing people hate it's a lawman who goes bad, and our readers are keen to hear the whole story. An interview with the man who made the arrest would be quite a scoop for me, if you could spare me a moment of your time.'

Ketteridge grunted but he looked flattered.

'Most of the reporters we've had here wanted to talk to Mitchell,' he said.

'Did you let them?'

'Nope. Court made its decision, there's nothin' more to be said. Scaffold's finished, hanging takes place day after tomorrow. In fact I'd say you're here a week too late, story's old news by now.'

'But there's still the execution,' the young man said. 'Justice, being seen to be done. That's why I'm here, Sheriff, to ensure that a guilty man gets what's coming to him.'

4

Palmer glanced out of the office window.

'It looks like quite a crowd gathering.'

'They've been comin' in all week,' Sheriff Ketteridge said. 'Seems a lot of folk are eager to see a lawman with a noose around his neck.'

'Well,' Palmer said reasonably, 'it's not that common. Something to pass on to their grandchildren. That's why I'd like to tell our readers your story. What do you say?'

With a shrug Ketteridge gestured to the chair opposite him and Palmer sat down, taking a notebook and pencil from his pocket. 'I appreciate this, Sheriff, I really do. I gather you found Aaron Stein's body?'

'That's right. I noticed there was still a lamp burning in the bank though it was daylight. The blinds were down and the door was locked. I broke in and found Aaron Stein stone cold, face down with his brains spread all over the floor, and the safe standin' wide open and empty. We had the clerk go through the accounts. He reckoned there was just over ten thousand dollars missing.'

'Stein was murdered sometime during the night; wasn't the shot heard?'

'Serenity's kind of a lively town. The hands from the Lazy T were havin' a party just along the street in the Ace of Spades. But once folks thought about it next day we figured out he'd been killed around ten o'clock.'

'And you worked out Bill Mitchell was the murderer, though he'd been county sheriff for a long time. A well-respected lawman wouldn't be the most obvious suspect.'

Ketteridge's brows furrowed.

'Guess not. But he didn't turn up at the office that day, I had to send Ethan to find him.'

'Ethan? I don't recall seeing that

name in the trial transcript.'

'Ethan Jones. He's a deputy.'

Palmer turned back through his notebook.

'I've got your name here as a deputy working for Mitchell, along with Mike Watts and Nathaniel Grimes. Looks like I missed something.'

'Jones wasn't a deputy then, he just fetched and carried, kept the place clean. I needed an extra man when I was made sheriff. It ain't just Serenity we take care of, it's a big chunk of territory.'

'Of course. Go on, you were saying Bill Mitchell didn't come to work.'

'That's right. Next thing, Gus Haller-field says he saw the sheriff go into the bank the night before. That's when I started thinkin' maybe Mitchell had been involved, and when Ethan fetched him he looked kinda queer.'

'Queer?' Palmer's eyebrows lifted. 'How?'

'First off I thought he'd spent the night drinking,' Ketteridge said. 'But

Ethan took a look at Mitchell's horse and it was covered in sweat like it had been ridden real hard.'

'How did Mitchell explain that?'

'He didn't. Said he'd been sick as a poisoned dog an' didn't remember a thing since the night before. He stuck to that story right through the trial. Bank's none too pleased, don't figure they'll ever see their money again.'

'The townspeople must have been shocked to find their sheriff was crooked.'

'Some of 'em.' Ketteridge said. 'But some wasn't surprised. They say Mitchell's a changed man since his wife died two years back.'

Palmer's pencil stopped scratching at the paper for a second, then he nodded abruptly and went on writing.

'You weren't friends.'

'He was a hard man to know,' Ketteridge said. 'He never talked more'n he had to. Anyways, soon after I'd seen Hallerfield two more witnesses came forward. They saw Mitchell and they heard the shot.'

Palmer nodded. 'I read about that. I'd say their evidence won the prosecution's case.' He consulted his notes again. 'Daisy Salmon and Rufus Corder both swore they heard Mitchell call out to Stein, and that Stein opened the door to him. The shot came no more than a few minutes later. That doesn't leave much room for doubt.'

'No. Mitchell offered no alibi.'

'Strange he didn't think of that when he planned the robbery. He lives alone?'

'Yeah. Reckoned he was doing his night rounds but took sick to his stomach when he was leavin' the Ace of Spades. Said he spent half the night in the shit-house out back, then slept till Ethan woke him.' Ketteridge said.

'Did he eat something bad? I don't recall if that question was asked at the trial.'

'The night of the robbery we all had the same food sent over from the hotel. Beef and tomatoes. There was a prisoner in the cells, name of Spurs

Osgood, he had it too, but none of us was sick. Hell, I never get sick.'

Palmer paused in his writing to look across at Ketteridge; the man was about the same height and build as himself, but at least fifteen years older. He had a round head sparsely covered with greying hair, and his body was solid and well-muscled, not yet running to fat.

'So Mitchell was placed under arrest. And none of the money was ever found.'

'Not a cent. We figure he took it out of town and hid it someplace. If he was up all night that would account for him bein' asleep when Ethan went callin'.'

'Thank you, Sheriff, you've been a great help. Only a couple more things. There have been rumours that somebody's trying to get Mitchell a reprieve, maybe even a pardon. If that fails do you fear an attempt at a jail-break?'

Ketteridge snorted. 'Quentin Jefferson's the owner of the Lazy T, friend of Mitchell's from way back. He insists Mitchell was set up; headed East a few days ago, said he'd take the case to the President if he had to.' He shook his head. 'He's wasting his time. And you don't need to worry about no jail-break, Mitchell's going to the scaffold day after tomorrow.'

Palmer nodded as he scribbled a note into his book.

'Thanks, Sheriff, I'll quote you. The judge, Winterson isn't it? Does he live in Serenity?'

'Sure, right at the head of Main Street, big house with a picket fence.' Ketteridge said.

'What about the witnesses? Where would I find them?'

'Daisy Salmon lives close by the bank. Hickory Salmon's the under-taker, an' he was none too pleased to find out his daughter was seeing Rufe Corder, but the pair of 'em said their piece on the witness stand fair enough. Gus Hallerfield runs the livery, he's easy to find.' He grimaced. 'Wouldn't try talking to Rufe just now, he don't take gettin' beat too well.'

'Few men do,' Palmer said. 'You won't mind if I speak to your deputies?'

'Go ahead. Mike's outside. Ethan Jones should be here in a couple of hours.'

The deputy, leaning against a post on the sidewalk, wore a yellow shirt stretched tight over his big belly; it caught the sun, eclipsing the tin star on his chest. He pulled a pouch from his pocket and bit off a chunk of tobacco.

'Mike Watts?' Palmer queried.

The big man nodded.

'Sheriff Ketteridge says I can ask you some questions,' Palmer said, looking up at the raw-boned face, the jaw working rhythmically. 'You got any objection?'

Watts shrugged and spat accurately on to a heap of horse-shit.

'Nothin' to do but watch the street,' he said. 'But if you're after makin' a show outa Bill Mitchell, I got nothin' to say.'

'You've known him a long time?'

'Twenty years. An' he'd no more rob

47

a bank an' murder a friend than I'd sit down in the street an' eat that.' He spat, hitting the target dead centre again.

'But there was a lot of evidence against him. What do you think happened?'

'Mister, I don't know. If I did I coulda done somethin' to help the sheriff at the trial.'

'To help Mitchell you mean.'

'Far as I'm concerned Serenity's only got one sheriff an' it sure as hell ain't Slim Ketteridge.'

'Were you on duty the night Stein was murdered?' Palmer asked.

'Yeah. Me and Bill left the office at the same time. Most nights he'd check the south end of town on his way home.' He shifted the quid to his other cheek. 'I turned north.'

'Before that you all had a meal. Who fetched it?'

'Ethan Jones.' Watts sent a jet of brown liquid splatting expressively on to the street. 'Wasn't a deputy then. Bill Mitchell never give him a badge.'

'Why not?'

'You'll see when you meet him,' Watts said. 'Ethan brought the food an' handed it around. Just before me an' the sheriff left he took the tray over to the hotel, then came back to share guard duty with Slim.'

'So all the men who could have tampered with the sheriff's food have an alibi for that night? None of you could have gone to the bank.'

'Looks that way.'

'And everybody else ate their meal? Nobody complained of feeling ill?'

'Nope, not so's I recall.' Watts sighed and spat disconsolately, abandoning his target and making a wet stain on the boards close by his feet. He heaved his big frame upright and nodded at a diminutive bow-legged figure crossing the street. 'I'm done for the day, that there's Nat Grimes come to take over here.'

'Grimes wasn't in town the night of the murder.'

'Nope. He was over to Sunset Ridge.

But he'll swear Bill's innocent, same as me. You gonna put that in your story?'

'I'm afraid a man's opinion doesn't carry much weight in law. Thank you for your time, Mr Watts.' Palmer ducked his head and stepped off the sidewalk, crossing the street with the scarred side of his face towards the approaching deputy who glanced curiously at him as he passed.

As he stepped up to the hotel doorway Palmer found his way barred by a group of cowboys. He was once again confronting Buck, but this time there was no smile on the weathered face.

'We got a few questions to ask you, mister.'

A hand reached to grab Palmer's bag, and his elbows were gripped from behind, fingers digging hard into his flesh. His feet were almost lifted off the ground. 'We'll just head down behind the saddlers here, so we won't inconvenience nobody.'

'I take it this isn't about my hat,'

Palmer said, assessing his chances of breaking free and coming up with a zero. By way of answer Buck whipped the derby off his head and flung it to the ground before them. Palmer saw a boot stamp on it, then it vanished in the cloud of dust raised by their passing.

They hustled him into an alleyway leading to a deserted barn. A dusty sign on the front declared it as the property of HUCKLE & MILLER DRY-GOODS. Palmer tried to turn himself around, kicking out with one heel and hearing a grunt as his boot connected with flesh, but it was no more than a token resistance.

'Quit that. Stop him, Cal.' Something hit Palmer hard along the side of his head and he winced at the pain of it. He put all his strength into one desperate lunge for freedom, tearing an arm free and bringing his elbow into one man's face, then lashing out with his fist to knock down a second. The cowboy they called Joe was suddenly in front of him, mouth open and eyes wide with excitement as he lashed out. Palmer couldn't see what he held in his hand but it came sweeping down to hit him on the temple. Lightning flashed in front of his eyes and his ears rang as he staggered under the blow, then they were all over him, an undisciplined rabble with hands grabbing, fists and feet pummelling him wherever they could reach. A fist adorned with a bunch of rings hit his scarred cheek and blood trickled down his jaw.

For the third time he was hit on the skull and this time Palmer lost the struggle to keep his brain from closing down. The voices of the men around him distorted as if they were shouting down a barrel and the day turned slowly into night. He drifted, spiralling through a long black tunnel, and then there was silence.

5

He was blind. Terror turned his guts to water and sent spasms rippling through his limbs. The illusion lasted no more than a second. It was an old nightmare, as old as the scar on his cheek; he'd lain at the bottom of a cliff with his eyes filled with blood and been sure he'd never see daylight again. With a shudder of relief he knew this darkness belonged to the night. Now he was a man, not a frightened child.

By turning his head Palmer found he could see stars swaying above him, magnifying the queasy motion of his body and the pounding of his back and skull against something hard. Another second and he'd worked out he was lying in a wagon that was lurching too fast over rough ground. The driver was a vague, hunched figure who was keeping his seat with difficulty, the reins looped around his hands as he alternately cursed and coaxed the horses.

Attempting to push himself to a sitting position, Palmer realized his wrists and ankles were tied. The discovery recalled him to the present; he might not know where he was, but he knew how he'd got there. His body ached; Buck and the boys had made quite a job of their Western welcome. He flexed his legs, shuffling around until he was braced into a corner; it wasn't much of an improvement, but his head was no longer crashing into the wagon bed with every jolt.

He lifted his bound hands to his mouth and began exploring the knotted rope with sore and swollen lips. Tugging with his teeth he pulled an end free. He had no idea why the cowboys had attacked him but he didn't intend to wait around and find out. It was slow work pulling at the knots by the uncertain starlight, and half the time he couldn't be sure whether he was loosening the rope or tightening it.

'Keep 'em movin', we gotta be back before dawn.'

Palmer froze. The voice came from uncomfortably close. A shape loomed against the stars to his right; Buck's horse moved at an easy lope alongside the jolting wagon.

'Why go so far?' the driver grumbled, taking a pull at the off-sider and swearing. 'We'll be crossin' the river soon, all we gotta do is tip him out.'

'And have him float down to town in the mornin' trussed up like a turkey-cock? Don't figure the boss'd be too happy about that.'

'We want rid of him, don't we?'

'Not that way. Use your brain, Cal, if you got one. You wanna think, try thinkin' about gettin' this team up the hill. We do this the way I said.'

Buck chirped to his horse and rode on, the sound of hoofs soon lost in the rumble of the wagon wheels. Palmer tore at the rope around his wrists, using his teeth like a wild animal caught in a trap, ripping flesh in his haste and tasting blood, metallic on his tongue, painfully aware of the passage of time.

The wagon went into the river, splashing water high so some of it landed on Palmer's face. He licked the cold spray off his lips and came back to his senses. He worked steadily at the knot with his mouth until he was able to slip a hand free, though he lost more skin in the process. Once he'd untied his legs he lay low, bouncing bruisingly around on the wooden boards, swallowing his curses and imagining getting his hands on Buck; he'd make the cowboy pay for every rut in that road.

Cautiously Palmer raised his head to look out. There was a solitary rider behind the wagon. His dark horse was almost invisible apart from the small white star on its forehead. He was too far behind; Palmer couldn't jump him, but even in the darkness it wasn't likely he'd miss seeing their prisoner throwing himself out over the side of the wagon. That wasn't an option Palmer favoured, leaping blindly into space, particularly as the wagon was climbing steadily and he could hear the river somewhere below.

His best chance was the driver. He could knock him out and get his hands on a gun, then deal with the man riding sweep. But as he knelt to bring his clubbed hands down on the man's neck Palmer saw Buck; the cowboy hadn't ridden far and he wasn't alone. There were four riders in a loose group on the pale ribbon of road that stretched ahead. Palmer flung himself flat again, landing hard and biting off an involuntary yell as the side of his head hit wood.

Seconds passed. A minute perhaps. He hadn't been seen, they didn't know he was free. The wagon was slowing, the horses barely jogging as the hill grew steeper. After a moment Palmer risked a look. The road here clung to the side of the valley. On the left a bare slope stretched up towards the starlit sky; that way he'd be totally exposed to view, but to the right there was a steep drop, scattered with rocks and stunted trees and patches of scrub. Far below water glimmered. Palmer bit down on his bruised lip. He didn't want to go that way, but nor did he want to wait and see how Buck intended to dispose of him.

Without giving himself time for second thoughts, he rose to his feet and grabbed the back of the driver's seat to half-leap, half-vault over the side of the wagon.

He hadn't seen the boulder standing squat and dark at the side of the road, and he missed smashing on to it with nothing to spare, his knee scraping against the rough stone. His feet scrabbled for purchase at the roadside. Arms windmilling as the drop yawned blackly before him he wavered on the brink. Somebody yelled and there was no more time.

Palmer plunged down the slope, letting his weight carry him, kept upright by little more than his sheer reluctance to fall, finding a route between barely seen trees and half-buried boulders that lay waiting to trap his feet. Running, sliding and jumping by turns, he descended towards the river, each step bringing a reminder of the beating Buck and his boys had delivered. From somewhere behind him their shouts followed him down, angry and urgent.

'Stop him!'

'Where'd he go? Reckon you didn't tie those knots too good.'

'Dammit Joe, you ridin' with your eyes shut? What d'you think you was there for?'

That was Buck. So it had been Joe behind the wagon. Palmer wished he'd been close enough to jump him. It would have been good to dish out a little repayment for that knock to the head. He felt like he'd had the same treatment as his derby hat, run down and flattened by pounding feet.

The river was close now, silver in the starlight. Skidding to a halt behind a tree with his boots almost in the shallows, Palmer stared at the water, thankful to have got this far unscathed. He bent to pick up a rock that lay at his feet and tossed it into the river; it sounded enough like a man diving in to fool the men high above. A broken tree-branch floated sluggishly against his boot and with sudden inspiration Palmer stepped down on the saturated wood, then released it; the few sodden leaves clinging to the other end came out of the water and dropped back with a muted splash. Gauging the distance across the river he repeated the action, quick but rhythmic; judging that a dozen strokes of his arms would have pulled him to the other side.

'He's swum across!' Buck sounded furious. 'You three head back down to the crossing, the slope's easier that side. He can't move fast on foot. And don't lose him.'

'Maybe we'd best let him go.'

'You was the one thought he was our man, Dawson. You changin' your tune now?'

'Didn't find no rope in that bag of his,' Dawson said. 'They say they always carry their own rope.'

'Coulda left it with the sheriff,' another man said. 'It's gotta be him. He went straight to the jail soon as he got off the train.'

'No use arguin',' Buck cut in. 'Right or wrong we gotta find him. Go on, get movin'. Cal, take the wagon to the ridge an' wait there. An' keep your eyes open. C'mon, Joe, we'll make sure he don't double back.'

'We ain't ridin' down there,' Joe protested.

'I wasn't plannin' to,' Buck said. 'You got two legs, don't you?'

'Sure, but that don't beat four.'

Palmer waited, listening. Three horses went galloping back the way the wagon had come, and the vehicle rumbled slowly on up the hill, while from the top of the slope there were sounds of a horse scuffing the dust. Palmer imagined it circling on the road, as reluctant as Joe to make the precarious descent. It had been a terrifying trip on foot, he could hardly believe anyone would be fool enough to try it on horseback.

A dark shadow tipped over the skyline. Palmer saw it silhouetted against the stars, then the horse was sliding, plunging with its head in the air, snorting a protest as it lost its footing and collapsed back on its haunches. He didn't see what happened after that; perhaps the beast hit a tree. There was a crash followed by a screaming neigh, and the horse came plummeting down the last of the slope on its back, to roll into the water a few yards from where Palmer stood. It lay on its side for a few seconds, then stood up, splay-legged and shaking.

The rider came a few seconds behind his mount, slithering through the dirt head first. He hit a tree ten feet above the river with a sickening thud, bounced off and slithered along bonelessly until he fetched up against the horse's legs. The beast threw up its head in renewed terror and Palmer noticed the small light mark between its eyes as it shied and reared away in a starlit burst of spray. An arrow of white water in the dark showed where it swam, then it was racing up the opposite bank to vanish between the trees, only an echo of its passing left behind.

Joe was dead. The tree had smashed his skull, leaving his thin face mis-shapen and one side of his straggly moustache angling bizarrely upwards, while a thin trickle of blood, black in the uncertain light, oozed from a dent above his eye.

'Joe?' Buck was descending the drop on foot, working his way warily from tree to tree, rock to rock.

'Down here,' Palmer said, bending to take the six-gun from the dead man's holster.

'That you, dude?'

'It's me. Joe can't answer for himself.' Palmer moved away from the body into deeper shadow.

'What you do to him?' Buck was close now, easing down the last steep slope.

'Nothing. He hit a tree. I doubt if any horse alive could keep its feet on a drop like that.' Palmer retreated a little further and watched as Buck leant over Joe's body to close the dead man's staring eyes, then he slowly cocked the gun. 'Unless you want to join Joe, you might want to toss your gun belt into the river, he said.

Buck turned, staring into the darkness.

'You shoot me an' the boys'll come runnin',' he said, his right hand moving slowly towards his belt buckle.

'Left hand,' Palmer said. 'I may be a dude but I'm not a fool. Into the water,' he added, as Buck stood with the belt dangling from his grasp. The cowboy threw the gun belt behind him and there was a loud splash.

'Now what?' Buck said.

'Now you tell me why you bush-whacked me. Then I decide whether to repay you for that sample of western hospitality you and your friends handed out.'

'Figured you'd have guessed, mister. We was hopin' to stop the hangin'. We was expectin' Mr Jefferson on the train today but he didn't show, so we made a move on our own. If you wasn't there they'd have to find another hangman, an' that'd give the boss time to think of a way to save the sheriff.'

There was a silence as Palmer digested what Buck said.

'You thought I was here to put the rope around Bill Mitchell's neck?' He gave a short humourless bark of laughter. 'Well, why not? I suppose I look the part.'

'You sayin' we got you wrong? Nat Grimes swore Ketteridge was expectin' the man off the midday train, an' you was sure in a hurry to get to the jail. If you ain't the hangman then why d'you come to Serenity?'

'To see justice done,' Palmer said. 'I believe in justice, even when it takes a lifetime.' From across the river there were sounds of approaching horses. 'I think it's time to go. We'll climb back up to the road. You first. And mind you don't fall.'

'What about Joe?'

'Your friends can pick him up. He won't mind waiting.'

6

Climbing to the top of the slope took a lot longer than hurtling down it, and by the time Palmer had prodded Buck up to the dusty road he could hear a commotion below them; the three men who'd been sent to ford the river had discovered Joe's body. Their voices echoed across the valley as they shouted for Buck, and the cowboy eyed his captor uneasily. 'Don't know what you're plannin',' he said, breathing hard. 'The boys'll be some mad about Joe.'

'I didn't kill him.'

'I know it but they don't. Be kinda stupid to make things worse.'

'You started this, not me,' Palmer said. 'You owe me for that beating, but nobody else needs to get hurt tonight. Just do me a couple of favours.'

'What favours?'

'Lend me your horse. And you can tell your friends I'm not the hangman.' Left-handed he explored the ruins of his jacket; one sleeve was torn almost clean off and the front had two new openings where they served no useful purpose. 'And I'll take your coat and hat.'

'Guess that's fair,' Buck said, reluctantly easing out of his coat and tossing it over.

'Count yourself lucky your pants wouldn't fit me,' Palmer said. 'These clothes were meant for city living.'

Buck gave him a long hard look.

'Maybe you ain't no executioner but I got a feelin' you ain't tellin' me the whole truth. Whose side are you on, mister?'

'I told you, I believe in justice. Do we have a deal? I'll leave your horse at the livery yard.'

'No, Gus ain't got no room with so many folks in town. I'll pick him up from the blacksmith's, that's if you can find your way back to Serenity,' Buck said. 'Give the horse its rein if'n you're lost an' he'll take you to the Lazy T.'

Palmer swung himself on to the horse, a neat little pinto that snorted at the feel of a different rider and seemed inclined to stand on its hind legs. Palmer gentled it.

'Nice horse,' he said, the ghost of a grin on his face as the animal quieted. 'I'll take good care of him.'

With that he spun the pinto around and headed back down the trail at a gallop, rousing new cries of alarm from the men wading around in the river at the bottom of the gully. He thought he heard Buck calling to them, but then there was only the rush of the wind in his ears and the pounding of hoofs beneath him.

The pinto splashed through the ford, hesitating only a moment when Palmer turned it on to a side trail that followed the course of the river downstream. He turned again, this time on to a deer-trod where the trees grew thick and close and he had to ease the animal to a walk and let out the rein so it could pick its way. No starlight pierced the canopy of leaves above.

A grassy shelf showed up as a lighter patch in the darkness, the river murmuring softly just out of sight below. Palmer lit down wearily and untied the slicker behind Buck's saddle. He loosened the cinches and looped the pinto's rein around a tree-branch so it could browse. With Buck's hat and coat for a pillow and the slicker for a bedroll Palmer lay down and was instantly asleep.

* * *

In the dawn cold Palmer rolled over and sat up. A haze of damp mist hung over the river and spread its tentacles through the trees. Easing through the pain of stiffened bruises he gathered wood and lit a fire; Buck hadn't been carrying food but there was a battered tin pot hanging from his saddle and coffee in a screwed-up packet. The coffee tasted good, but it reminded Palmer that it was twenty-four hours since he'd eaten. He washed the blood from his face and rubbed a tentative hand over the bristles sprouting from his chin, then he put on Buck's coat over his own, adjusted the cowboy's hat on his head and led the pinto alongside a fallen tree so he could heave himself painfully into the saddle.

The boundary of the Corder ranch was identified by the skull of a steer lodged in the fork of a dead tree, both seared so white by the sun it looked like the bones had grown there. When asked to pass this marker the pinto made a brief objection as if it knew it was entering enemy territory; Palmer clapped his heels to its sides and flicked the rein against its neck and with a snort the little horse leapt to a run, abandoning its attempt to turn homewards.

A ghostly stand of cottonwoods loomed out of the morning mist. A stag stood on its edge, neck-high in white vapour. Seeing him it started away just as a rifle shot cracked through the silence, the sound sending a handful of crows spiralling noisily into the air. A heavyset man erupted from among the trees on a big grey horse. The rifle held against his shoulder one-handed was aimed at Palmer as he came, the hard lines of his face heavily shadowed by the sun that had crept over the horizon.

'You just lost me a damn fine deer,' the man said. The horse stopped five yards from Palmer, halted by a backward jerk of the rider's head, for the reins were looped around his neck, his right arm hung useless at his side. His hat hung on its draw-tie so his head was bare, showing thick red hair grown long and unkempt over his ears.

'I'm sorry,' Palmer said. 'I'm on my way to see Rufus Corder, but perhaps it's a little early.'

'You're lookin' for brother Rufe?' The man stared at him, his brow furrowing. He lowered the rifle. 'I'm Rollo Corder. Heard there was a dude with a messed-up face in town. Seems somebody thought to mess it up some more.'

'That was the hands from the Lazy T,' Palmer said.

The man's eyes opened wider as he noticed the horse Palmer rode. He urged his own mount a few steps closer to look at the coat and hat he wore, then a savage grin lit his face.

'You may be a dude but I reckon you ain't wet behind the ears. What you do with Buck?'

'Left him to take some exercise. He can have the horse back when I've finished with it, but I may keep the clothes.'

Sliding the rifle into its scabbard Rollo held out his good hand. 'Mister, I figure Rufe'll be real happy to meet you.'

★ ★ ★

Talking had no place at the Corder's breakfast table. Twelve men sat around the long wooden boards down the

73

centre of the room, the only sound the clatter of eating-irons and an occasional belch. Rollo pushed two cowboys aside to make room for himself, pointing to a man who sat at the other side.

'There,' he said, already grabbing for the corn-bread as he sat down. Palmer looked across at the young red-haired man he'd seen fight Buck the day before, taking in the black eye and the split lip. Despite Rollo's assurance to the contrary, Rufe didn't look happy to see him.

'Mr Corder.' Palmer removed Buck's hat from his head and nodded to the man who sat at the top of the table, an older version of his sons though his hair was thin and faded compared to theirs. His face was set permanently into hard lines so it looked to be made up of angles, the pale-blue eyes mere chips under a crag of forehead. 'My name's Palmer. I hope you'll excuse me calling so early. I'd like a word with your son Rufus.'

'He tangled with the Lazy T an' beat

up on Buck,' Rollo said, his words coming round a mouthful of bacon. 'Got Buck's horse outside.' An old woman crept from a corner bearing a coffee-pot and Rollo thrust a mug at her. 'Here.'

'I'm Red Corder.' The older man paused in his chewing and nodded at the wall-eyed man seated at the other end of the table. 'Whitey, make room for our visitor. Sit down and join us, mister, then we'll talk. Martha, give him a plate. Where's the girl?'

The woman shrugged as she put a plate in front of Palmer.

'Ain't seen her,' she said.

Not another word was spoken for a solid quarter of an hour. Palmer made up for his involuntary fast the day before, shovelling corn-bread and bacon into his mouth with no more finesse than Rollo, ignoring the looks Rufe was sending in his direction.

After drinking his fourth refill Red Corder slapped his coffee mug down hard. As if at a signal the men rose and headed for the door, the one called Whitey leading the way. Only Rollo was still eating, having been late to table, while Rufe swung himself astride the bench and took the makings of a cigarette from his top pocket, his eyes on Palmer.

'What business you got with Rufe?' Red asked.

'I work for the *Eastern Gazette*,' Palmer replied, turning to thank the old woman as he refused the offer of more coffee, 'and I'm here to write about the Mitchell case. Nobody likes to see a lawman turn bad, but it makes a good story. People need to know that a murderer gets what's coming to him.'

'Oh, Mitchell's gonna get his right enough,' Rollo said. 'An' not before time.'

'You plannin' to sit there stuffin' your face till sundown?' Red snapped, jerking his head towards the door.

'Just goin',' Rollo said, standing up and dragging his right arm around with his left so it swung clear of the table. He nodded at Palmer. 'They string the sheriff up at noon tomorrow,' he said. 'We sure ain't fixin' to miss it.'

'You'll excuse my boy,' Red said as Rollo departed. 'It was Mitchell left him that way. Reckon it's providence that Rufe here was one of the witnesses when he shot the banker, kinda sets things fair.'

'You say the sheriff was responsible for your son's injury?' Palmer had his notebook out of his vest pocket and was reaching for a pencil. 'How did that happen?'

Red stared at him for a moment, his faded blue eyes calculating.

'The boys was havin' a bit of a disagreement with Jake Jefferson an' some of his friends,' he said. 'Jake's Quentin Jefferson's whelp, boss of the Lazy T. It wasn't nothin' too serious, they wasn't doin' no harm.'

'Rollo an' Whitey was doin' fine till the sheriff come along,' Rufe said. 'Mitchell, he never could stand us Corders, an' he pitched in to save

Jake's precious skin.'

'Mitchell never gave my son a chance,' Red growled. 'Plugged him in the shoulder without so much as stoppin' to haul a breath. Bullet damaged somethin' the doc couldn't mend, and that arm won't never be no use to him, might as well have taken it off, but the boy said he'd hold on to it, kind of a keepsake.'

'Reminds us all how it happened,' Rufe said. 'Though if I'd been wearin' a gun that day Mitchell would've died right there. Kinda glad now he didn't. Reckon it's better he's settin' in that cell waitin' on the hangman.' He grinned. 'Watchin' him swing tomorrow's gonna be real sweet.'

7

'I understand how your family feels about Mitchell,' Palmer said, watching Rufe Corder roll his second cigarette. 'But I've heard there are people who want the sentence changed.'

Hostile blue eyes met his through a spiral of smoke.

'Mitchell's set to hang, don't matter what folks think.'

'You were one of the key witnesses at Mitchell's trial,' Palmer said. 'Did anyone mention what happened to your brother?'

'The two things ain't connected,' Rufe said, the blue gaze turning colder.

'Of course not. But those who want a retrial will stir up any dirt they can. Discrediting your evidence would be a good start.'

'It's too late for 'em to do nothin'.' Red dismissed the idea with a wave of his hand. 'Serenity's got a new sheriff, an' he ain't gonna stand for no trouble tomorrow, he's got a whole passel of deputies sworn in, includin' me an' my boys.'

'There's only the Jeffersons likely to try anythin',' Rufe said, 'but Slim Ketteridge is gonna make sure Mitchell goes to the gallows, he ain't afraid of the Lazy T. Maybe they won't even turn up, maybe they don't have the guts to watch their friend get his neck stretched.'

'That's enough, boy,' Red growled. 'Mr Palmer's got better things to do than listen to you.'

Rufe stubbed out his cigarette on the sole of his boot and stood up.

'Then I'll git.'

'I only wanted to ask two more questions,' Palmer said. 'You were with Daisy Salmon in the alley alongside the bank that night. I suppose you'd met her there before?'

'Sure, a dozen times. Daisy's a real pretty girl.' Rufe smiled but his eyes were still cold. 'Jake Jefferson was fixin' to marry her, but he wasn't treatin' her right an' the girl needed a shoulder to cry on. Needs it even more now he's ditched her.'

'And you and Daisy both saw the sheriff walk across to the bank, and you both heard him call out to the man inside?'

'Yeah. Go ask Daisy, she was real upset when that sister of hers made her tell Ketteridge about it,' Rufe said. 'But hell, we couldn't keep it quiet, wouldn't be right, not when a man was killed an' all.'

'You heard the shot, the one that killed Stein?'

'Sure did.' He smirked. 'Me an' Daisy was kinda busy right then, though if I'd knowed what was happenin' I would've took a look-see.'

Palmer rose to his feet and thanked Red Corder for the meal.

'Any man who picks a fight with the Lazy T is welcome in my house,' the old man said. 'Rufe, see him to his horse.'

Palmer paused in the doorway and turned to Rufe again.

'Now Daisy Salmon's no longer engaged I imagine you can see her any time you wish?'

'Guess I could at that, but I won't. I got me a wife.' Rufe walked out to the hitching-rail with him. Palmer untied the pinto, wincing at the need to use torn muscles as he tightened the cinches. 'I sure hope Buck's as sore as you are, mister,' Rufus said.

Before Palmer could reply a horse exploded out through the open door of the barn, a streak of pale gold galloping for the open prairie. A girl sat the palomino as if she'd been born in the saddle; she wore a man's jacket that flapped loosely around her as she rode, and her head was covered by a man's hat with the brim turned down until the speed of her flight tore it off to bounce against her back in the wind.

'Hey, she's on my horse!' Rufe shouted. 'Git back here, girl!'

Palmer had a brief glimpse of a pale

face topped with a dark mane of hair that caught the sun in deep red shades like the embers of a dying fire. Then horse and rider were gone, shape and sound blurred in the cloud of dust they left behind. A shiver ran up his spine. He felt as if the world had just taken a side-step without him, leaving him uneasily adrift.

Rufe snatched the reins out of his hand and was halfway into the saddle. Palmer linked his hands together beneath Rufe's left foot and heaved, sending him flying right over the pinto's back to land heavily on the other side. The horse took a step backwards. Palmer retrieved his reins then stepped up and into the saddle so nearly occupied by Rufe.

Red came out of the house to stare after the disappearing horse.

'What the hell?'

'That bitch just rode out of here on my horse,' Rufe snarled, coming up fast and charging towards Palmer, who had the pinto backing away. 'I need that pinto, I gotta get after her.'

'Don't be a fool, boy.' Red's gaze shifted from his son to Palmer and back again. 'You want to borrow a man's ride you ask him polite.'

'But she took my horse,' Rufe protested. 'That girl's askin' for a whippin'.'

'Maybe so, but there's plenty more mounts in the corral,' Red said. 'Women was made for chasin' son, but it ain't no sport unless they got a head start.' He chuckled, looking at Palmer. 'The girl's my brother's daughter. Pretty sassy, ain't she? Reckon the boy here could be bitin' off more'n he can chew. Like takin' a wildcat to bed.'

'Apparently he has to catch her first,' Palmer said.

Rufe swore and shouted for one of the hands to saddle a horse, throwing Palmer a malevolent sidelong glance.

'Thank you again for the breakfast, Mr Corder.' Palmer touched Buck's hat and rode away, the horse jogging beneath him, seemingly eager to leave the place behind. By the dead tree with its melancholy pointer Palmer hesitated; the pinto wanted to take him to the Lazy T and it was a place he knew he must visit before long, but from what Buck had said Quentin Jefferson wouldn't be home. With sudden purpose he turned the horse towards Serenity and pushed it to a gallop.

The trail passed through a scattering of boulders, the morning sun casting long shadows beneath them. The palomino's bright coat shone as it stepped out into his path, the girl reining in as though she'd been waiting for him, though she'd put the hat back on and the brim hid her features. She kept her head tilted down, pretending to find something interesting in the darkness beneath the rocks.

Palmer's mouth twisted in its sardonic smile; he was used to women not caring to look at his face.

'Rufe won't be far behind me,' he said. 'You'd better ride on unless you want him to catch you.'

'I can deal with Rufe,' she said. Her voice was low for a woman, and the sound warmed him. He bit down on the feeling; this girl was married to young Corder. Even so he pushed the pinto forward to get a closer look but with the briefest shift of her weight she turned the palomino and he was left staring at the long mane of dark hair draped across her shoulder, reflecting the sun like burnished copper. It was hard to guess her shape beneath the man's jacket but her hand on the rein was pale and slender. 'I saw you ride in with Rollo,' she said. 'Why did you come?'

He had the feeling she was asking more than just the reason of his visit to the Corder ranch.

'To ask Rufe some questions,' he said.

She nodded. 'About the sheriff. That's what I thought. That's why I had to talk to you. Rufe hasn't told you the truth, he knows more than he's telling.'

'Are you saying he and the girl told lies in court?'

'I don't know, Red and the boys are careful what they say in front of me. But I heard they've made a deal with Slim Ketteridge. And they've been taking on more hands.'

Palmer nodded slowly.

'Four of the men sitting down to breakfast weren't cowboys. But what would the Corders want with hired guns?'

'That's easy,' she said. 'They've got the chance at last to push the Jeffersons into a fight. Once Bill Mitchell's dead there won't be anyone to stop them taking over the open range on the far side of the river.' Her head turned for the briefest moment, but the hat hid her face. 'Rufe's coming.'

Palmer looked round. A cloud of dust showed where a rider was racing along the trail towards them.

'He'll see you as soon as you leave the shadows.'

'It's best he doesn't know we met,'

she said. 'Stay here and don't come after me.' She pushed the palomino out into the light, turning it towards the open prairie.

'Wait,' Palmer said. 'Why did you tell me all this?'

'Because I know who you are.' The words came back to him on the wind as she sprang the horse to a gallop. The hat flew off again, revealing the full glory of her hair. The moving shape that was Rufe Corder changed course to go after her, and Palmer watched as the distance between them shortened. Rufe rode a big rangy black, and it was fast; though the girl rode well it was a race she couldn't win. Against his inclination Palmer stayed in the shadows, but then the black overtook the palomino and both vanished inside a whirling dust cloud.

The ghost of a big riderless horse emerged jogging uneasily towards him, head up and tail swinging, followed a moment later by the paler shape of the palomino. Palmer could see nothing of

Rufe or the girl. Rufe's wife, he reminded himself. He swore and slapped his heels into the little pinto's ribs, leaning low as the horse flattened, eating up the ground. He took off Buck's hat and waved it at the two loose horses, shouting to turn them. They halted and veered in alarm, circling together as he passed.

Through the dust Palmer saw Rufe lying on top of the girl, his right hand drawing back to strike her across the face; his other fist closed round her two wrists, pinioning them above her head. She bucked beneath him, trying to throw him aside, not cowed by his brutality, screaming not in terror but in defiance.

Rufe laughed aloud then he ripped at the girl's shirt, his hand groping for her breast. She spat and he jerked his head back. In that split second when his grip eased she pulled her hands free and at once she was gouging at his eyes with her fingers. He howled and rolled away from her but she followed, scrabbling after him on all fours and throwing a handful of dust into his contorted face.

'You think I'd ever marry you?' The girl yelled. 'I'd sooner take your horse to bed!' Getting to her feet she aimed a kick at his ribs. It was a stupid move; despite being blinded Rufe had the use of his hands and he grabbed at her foot, throwing her like a maverick. He hurled his whole weight on to her body, grinding her into the dirt, his hands seeking out her arms to pin her again, then he hitched himself higher so her face was beneath his chest, his boots thudding into her legs.

Lying low on the pinto's neck Palmer bore down on them. He heaved on its mouth, the animal sending a spray of dirt into the air as it slid on its haunches. It came to a halt with its forefeet only inches away from the struggle taking place on the ground. Palmer flung himself out of the saddle and grabbed Rufe's hair, pulling his head back and up. Twisting so he could see who held him Rufe howled a curse, pure rage glaring up at Palmer out of the bloodshot eyes. The girl squirmed away from them on hands and knees, choking on the dust.

Wriggling like an eel and lightning-fast Rufe swept a hand up to chop at Palmer's wrist, tearing himself free. He rolled and was swiftly on his feet, then he came with hands grasping for the throat, the speed of his attack bearing Palmer to the ground. Long sinewy fingers dug deep into his neck. Palmer's hands clawed at the powerful wrists but Rufe grinned savagely and squeezed a little harder.

8

No air was reaching Palmer's lungs. The growing darkness before his eyes was split by bright flashes of light shooting painfully through his head. His hands were round Rufe's wrists, which were fleshless and hard as knotted steel. Death was only moments away.

He hadn't come to Serenity to die. Flexing his broad shoulders he began to pull his hands apart. Little by little the pressure on his throat eased and he could see again. He dragged in a morsel of air.

'You're a dead man,' Rufe hissed.

'Not yet.'

Rufe's face contorted with rage as he fought to maintain his sinewy grip, but Palmer was winning, sheer muscular strength overcoming the advantage gravity gave to Rufe's attack. Breath was scorching down into Palmer's tortured lungs again and with a gargantuan effort he flung his arms wide. As Rufe's weight plummeted on to him he brought one knee up hard to take the younger man between the legs. Rufe screeched and took to the air. As he smacked into the ground Palmer scuttled breathlessly after him and dropped across the wiry body.

'My turn,' he gasped, his bunched fists slamming into Rufe's belly. The result was spectacular. A whistling choking groan came from Rufe's mouth and his face turned grey as a snow-laden sky.

The prairie whirled as Palmer struggled to his feet; it still hurt to breathe, and Rufe's treatment had done nothing to help the bruises left by the welcome he'd received from the Lazy T. He staggered into something and recoiled. It was the pinto; he'd collided with its flank, and the horse was there because the girl held its rein. She sat the palomino alongside, not hiding her face any more. As he stared her lips curved in a slight smile.

'Come on,' she ordered. He didn't obey at once, mesmerized by large eyes like bottomless pools in a perfect oval face only half-obscured by her rich mane of hair. Then his gaze moved down to take in the rest of her. A flush spread to colour her throat. Rufe had ripped her clothes right down to the skin and Palmer saw the tip of a wine-coloured nipple through a tear in her white bodice before she grabbed the front of her jacket and covered herself.

'Rufe claims you're his wife,' Palmer said. 'Tell me it's not true.'

She flushed even deeper but she met his eyes defiantly.

'Not if they hog-tie me,' she said. 'Though it's no business of yours.'

'I plan to make it my business,' he said.

Rufe was moving. He was on his knees, one hand groping for the knife in his belt. Recalling the way he'd so nearly finished Buck, Palmer backed

94

away, the girl's spell broken. He threw himself haphazardly at the pinto's saddle, hooking a knee around the horn, unable to get his weight over far enough to get astride. Rufe was on his feet, swaying towards them with the knife in his fist.

The girl thrust her knee under Palmer's thigh to push him into the saddle. Straightening, he grabbed at the reins but she was already hauling the pinto into motion; it whisked him away just as Rufe's blade came slashing at his arm, missing by inches. The two horses leapt to a gallop and raced across the prairie side by side, Palmer holding on to the pinto's mane to keep himself in the saddle, his right foot feeling for the iron. Now he was out of Rufe's reach every bone in his body was hurting. From behind them came the crack of half a dozen pistol shots.

At last the girl pulled up, the pinto's stride slowing in a succession of bone-jarring bucks that almost dislodged Palmer; only his reluctance to let his abused carcass hit the dirt keeping him from falling. He spat out trail dust and grabbed the reins as the girl threw them across the horse's neck.

'Town's that way,' she said, pointing.

'What about you?' he asked, frustrated to find she'd gone back to hiding her face from him. He wanted to see those amazing eyes again; he wanted to know if they were green or blue. 'I can't just ride away and leave you here.'

'Don't worry,' she said. 'Rufe's horse ran off, he won't be along for a while.'

'But he was shooting at you.'

She laughed bitterly.

'I don't think so, he still hopes to get me in his bed. You're the most likely target. I'd advise keeping out of his way till he cools down.'

'I will if you will,' he said. 'You won't go back to that house?'

For a moment there was silence.

'No,' she said, nudging the palomino into motion. When she spoke again she was already riding away. 'Get out of here.'

★　★　★

It was almost midday and uncomfortably hot when Palmer rode into town, with Buck's coat and the ruin of his own jacket slung across the saddle bow and Buck's hat angled low to keep the sun off his face. Serenity was so full of people it was hard to thread a path between them. Still more folk were arriving, mostly on horseback but some in buckboards or heavy wagons; he even saw a fancy two-wheeler pulled by a grey Arabian drawing up outside the hotel. Three men stared at him from the steps of a rundown saloon. He recognized them. They'd been among the ranch hands sitting at the Corder's breakfast table but these men didn't make a living punching cows. They wore fancy tooled gun belts, the holsters hanging low and tied down on their thighs.

Palmer looped the pinto's rein over the fence outside Judge Winterson's house and stepped up to the door, shrugging into Buck's coat. He'd stopped at a creek to wash his face and slick back his hair, but there wasn't much he could do about the bruises on his face and neck, or the trickle of blood that oozed persistently from his scarred cheek.

The woman who answered his knock looked Palmer up and down in obvious suspicion and left him standing on the step while she took his name inside. Returning a few moments later she sniffed as she reluctantly opened the door wide and ushered him into a book lined room.

'Mr Palmer.' Judge Winterson was younger than he'd expected, dark-haired and thin, his face pale as if he rarely went outside. He came forward to shake hands. 'Sheriff Ketteridge told me you were in town. I've been expecting you.' His eyes travelled swiftly over Palmer's face and clothes but he showed no surprise at his dishevelled state, waved him to a seat then sat down at his desk, leaning forward with his elbows on the polished leather surface, his hands steepled. 'Serenity doesn't often attract the attention of a newspaper like the *Eastern Gazette*. Tell me how I can help you.'

'As I explained to Sheriff Ketteridge, my editor sent me here to investigate the rumours that have been circulating ever since Mitchell was sentenced. A lot of people seem to think he won't hang. I'd like your view, Judge. Is it likely he'll be granted a last-minute reprieve?'

Winterson's brows drew together.

'Absolutely not. If that's the story you're hoping to write then you're wasting your time, Mr Palmer. There isn't going to be any last-minute drama. Mitchell has no chance of escaping the rope.'

'But the rumours must have started somewhere. Doesn't Mitchell have friends? I get the impression some people don't believe he's guilty, including the men who work at the Lazy T.' So much so they'd been prepared to kidnap the man they thought was due to hang him.

'Quentin Jefferson is the owner of the Lazy T,' Winterson said, 'which makes him one of the wealthiest and most influential men in these parts. He's known Mitchell a very long time. He's convinced of Mitchell's innocence, though he has no evidence to support his claim. We're expecting him back in town any time now. He rode to the state capital as soon as the verdict was made known, hoping to get a retrial. I assure you he won't succeed.'

'Mitchell's previous record as a lawman, doesn't that count for anything?'

'There's no precedent for remitting a sentence simply because a man is previously of good character,' Winterson said. 'Murder is still murder.' He sighed. 'Believe me, I deeply regretted imposing a death sentence, but I had no choice. The evidence was quite overwhelming, there were witnesses. Mitchell killed Aaron Stein and robbed the bank of over ten thousand dollars. He was found guilty, and he'll hang.'

'Are there any circumstances in which you'd change your mind? I'm sorry to keep going over the same ground, but I have to send back some kind of story. I assume you're the one person in Serenity with the authority to have the hanging stopped if anything new came to light.'

'It's true that if additional evidence was presented to me I'd be responsible for any investigation that seemed necessary. I could order a postponement of the sentence until that was done.'

'You think that's unlikely,' Palmer said.

'Very.' Winterson was blunt.

'Then if Mitchell's supporters want to help him the only thing they can do is break him out of jail.'

Winterson shook his head.

'I have every faith in Sheriff Ketteridge. He's a good man, and he's taken on extra deputies to ensure the rule of law is followed here. Anyone attempting to pervert the course of justice can expect the most severe penalty. If Quentin Jefferson is foolish enough to intervene he'll face a prison sentence.'

Palmer looked up from the notes he was writing.

'What's your personal opinion? Why do you think Mitchell went off the rails that way?'

'I don't know. I doubt if we'll ever understand what motivated the crime. Mitchell maintains he's innocent, despite the weight of evidence against him.' Winterson shrugged. 'It's not uncommon for criminals to take their secrets to the grave. Confession may be good for the soul but it will bring Mitchell no favours now, so it's unlikely we'll ever know what he did with the money. The bank isn't happy, of course, except to know that he'll pay the ultimate penalty.'

'An eye for an eye, a tooth for a tooth,' Palmer quoted, rising and offering his hand. 'An old sentiment but still valid. Thank you for your time, sir.'

'You're staying in town?'

'I haven't spoken to all the witnesses yet; even if there's no reprieve I have to file a story,' Palmer said.

'You might be wiser to depart today, there's an Eastbound train leaving at six.' The judge looked pointedly at the state of Palmer's clothes, and his face. 'Some of our people have evidently given you a rough time. I wouldn't like to see a visitor to Serenity get seriously hurt.'

Palmer glanced down at Buck's coat.

'I should have had the sense to blend in a little more with the surroundings when I arrived,' he said. 'Don't worry, Judge. After tangling with both the Lazy T and the Corders I've no intention of getting involved in any more arguments.'

9

A sign hanging alongside the barber's shop directed Palmer into a large yard. A house faced him, flanked by a workshop stacked with timber and coffins to the right, and a barn with doors standing open to reveal a shiny black hearse on the left. In sombre letters the hearse informed him he'd found Salmon's Undertaking Emporium. Between the barn and the barber-shop wall a narrow alleyway ran back towards Main Street.

'You lookin' for somethin'?' A man in an apron came out of the workshop, wiping his hands on a rag.

'I'd like a word with Mr Salmon.'

'He's in the house, though if it's business you can talk to me,' the man offered.

'Nobody died yet,' Palmer said.

Hickory Salmon was a dried-up little

man with hands that wrung constantly together with a faint rasping sound. He ushered Palmer into a neat parlour furnished in sombre brown. Black drapes framed the window. The undertaker called to some unseen presence from the door before he stepped inside.

'A pot of coffee, daughter.' He gave a funereal smile as he invited Palmer to sit down. 'What can I do for you, sir?'

'I'm talking to witnesses in the Mitchell case. I was hoping to see Miss Daisy Salmon.' A plain woman who could have been any age from twenty-five to forty entered carrying a tray. She set it down, poured coffee into two cups without looking at the men and went out.

'Would that be your daughter?'

'That's Violet. Daisy's my younger daughter.' Hickory Salmon frowned, his fingers and thumbs working hard. 'Most of the reporters left once the jury delivered its verdict. I find your interest distasteful, with the hanging due tomorrow.'

'I'm here to see justice done. Mitchell committed murder.'

'Did he? You're a stranger to Serenity Mr Palmer, yet you seem very sure of your facts. There are times when the truth can be elusive.' Salmon's hand-wringing became increasingly vigorous. 'Lots of people don't believe Bill Mitchell killed Aaron Stein.'

'Then they're ignoring the evidence,' Palmer said, drinking his coffee.

'Indeed. And you won't find many folk prepared to stand up and challenge that evidence publicly.' Salmon sighed. 'It's way too late now anyway.' He went to the door and called. 'Daisy, come in here.'

Daisy wasn't a bit like her sister. She dressed to make the most of her generous proportions, and her fair hair was elaborately curled. A wide flirtatious smile flashed in Palmer's direction as soon as she entered the room and it barely quivered when she saw his scarred face. Since women back East had been known to scream and faint when they met him, Palmer found himself returning the smile; Daisy was a pleasure to look at, and he felt inclined to disregard the fact that she doubtless greeted all men with equal enthusiasm.

'Daisy,' Salmon said, 'Mr Palmer wants to question you about the night Aaron Stein was killed.'

The young woman's tone was demure as she looked down at the floor and murmured:

'Yes, Papa. Violet said to tell you Mr Venables is here.'

Salmon wrung his hands together so hard the joints cracked.

'You'll excuse me, Mr Palmer, I have to see this man. I'll send Violet in.'

Palmer didn't speak until the older woman arrived, and Daisy too was silent, though she continued to look coyly at him through her lashes. As before, Violet Salmon didn't look directly at Palmer, merely offering him more coffee and sitting down close by her sister when he refused.

'Miss Daisy, may I ask how well you know Mr Mitchell?' said Palmer.

'Pretty well,' she replied. 'My father's on the law committee and they have meetings here now and then. If you're thinking I was mistaken about that night, it's not so, though it's a crying shame that a man like Mr. Mitchell should have to hang.'

'But you're quite sure of his guilt.'

'I don't know about that,' she replied pertly. 'All I know is, I heard Sheriff Mitchell call out to Mr. Stein, and I saw him go into the bank.'

'But it was dark. You couldn't actually see his face.'

'No.'

Palmer looked down at his notebook.

'At the trial the defence suggested it was just the sheriff's wide-brimmed hat you recognized.'

'Well, nobody else in town has one like it.' She looked at him in cool appraisal, not in the least upset by his questions. 'But I couldn't make a mistake about what I heard. He said:

'All right Aaron?' Just like the other times.'

'Other times? I don't think you mentioned any previous occasions in court.'

She shrugged, pushing a curl into place.

'I didn't want my father to know that it wasn't the first time I'd met Rufe in the alleyway.' She pouted, sending a glare in the direction of her sister. 'There was enough trouble without admitting I'd been seeing him for months. I wouldn't have said anything at all if Violet hadn't made me.'

'So you saw the sheriff walk into the bank. Then what happened?'

'We heard a shot. But we didn't realize that that was where it came from. There was a real ruckus going on in the Ace of Spades that night.'

'Did you and Rufe Corder stay in the alleyway after you heard the shot? Maybe you went on talking to each other,' Palmer said.

'I don't exactly recall,' she answered.

She looked down briefly at her fingers twisting together in her lap, the gesture a pale imitation of her father's. 'Yes, yes of course we did. Then after a while Rufe walked me back home.'

'And where did he go when he left you?'

'I guess he crossed the yard,' she said. 'He always tied his horse outside the barber's shop.'

'But you didn't see him go that way?'

'No.' She stilled her hands and folded them deliberately. 'I don't think this makes much of a story. Gus Hallerfield saw pretty much the same as we did, maybe you ought to talk to him.'

'I intend to.' Palmer put his notebook away and rose to his feet. 'Just one more thing you ladies might be able to tell me, I gather Mitchell's wife died. Does he have any other family? Wasn't there anyone who might have corroborated his version of events that night?'

'He has a daughter,' Violet said, pursing her thin lips. 'But she got married a year ago. She and her husband moved out to the old McEndry place.'

'I see,' he said. 'Thank you. You've both been very helpful.'

'Will you mention my name in your newspaper?' Daisy asked. Violet hushed her and escorted Palmer to the door.

'You'll excuse my sister's foolishness,' she said softly. 'You'll have heard she was engaged to another man when this happened. And of course, once I realized she'd been a witness to murder I had to tell my father. It wasn't my fault she was carrying on with two men at once.' She sounded smug.

'I'm sure Miss Daisy's like many pretty girls in that respect,' he said. 'She can hardly help attracting attention.'

Violet Salmon's eyes narrowed.

'You'd know about the importance of appearances, of course,' she hissed. She slammed the door shut behind him.

A boy of about twelve brought the pinto out of the barn. Palmer felt in his pocket for a coin and brought out a nickel. Then he paused and fished for a

111

quarter. The youngster's eyes widened.

'Would you be able to get a message to Miss Daisy for me?' Palmer asked. 'Right away? And without her sister or father knowing?'

'Yessir.' He winked. 'Do it all the time.'

'Then ask her to meet me in that alleyway as soon as it gets dark.' He handed over the coins and took the pinto's reins.

'Sure thing, mister. You can leave your horse by the barber's shop,' he added helpfully, 'or if there's no room you call in here an' I'll take care of him for you. No charge. Mr. Salmon spends his evenin's in the Golden Gate, he won't see nothin'.'

'It's not my horse,' Palmer replied. 'I have to return him to his owner, but thanks anyway. Can you direct me to the livery stables?'

Hallerfield's yard was overflowing with horses; there were animals tethered to every available space, and as Palmer approached with the pinto a big sorrel put its ears back and kicked out. Missing the pinto, one of the sorrel's hoofs hit a bay standing alongside and the bay side-stepped into a chestnut mare. The mare squealed and lashed out in her turn. Attacked from both sides the bay jerked back and broke its rein, wheeling free. A short plump figure shot out of the barn and caught the bay, cursing the sorrel and the mare.

'Pedro,' he roared, 'you idle no-good sonofabitch, didn't I tell you to keep an eye on things out here?'

A dark-skinned man slouched from behind another line of horses.

'Can't be every place at once,' he muttered, grabbing the bay's rein.

'Worse'n the fourth of July,' the plump man grumbled, turning to Palmer. 'Don't know as I can take one more horse, never seen this town so darn full.'

'I wasn't planning to leave him. My name's Palmer, I'm from the *Eastern Gazette*. I was hoping for a word with you, Mr Hallerfield. Perhaps I could buy you a drink.'

'Best idea I've heard all damned day. Pedro, find a place for the pinto.' He led the way out through the back of the yard, scattering a handful of chickens and a pig, ducking through a broken fence and skirting round the ruin of a wagon that stood on a rubbish heap. 'No use goin' in through the street today,' he explained, pushing his way through a creaking door into a dark kitchen. 'Take an hour to get served.'

A woman looked up from a sink and nodded.

'Bottle's on the table, Gus. Leave the money in the jar.'

'Thanks, Mary.' He picked up a couple of glasses from those she'd washed and ushered Palmer through another door into a small dingy room that held nothing but a table and four chairs. On the table stood a bottle, and a jar half-full of coins. Palmer tossed a handful of small change into the jar as Hallerfield poured.

'Your health Mr Palmer,' Hallerfield said, tossing off the first glassful and helping himself to another, grinning as Palmer took a cautious sip then an appreciative swallow. 'Mary saves the best for her regular customers. That's whiskey the way it should be; goes down smooth as silk then kicks like a mule.' There was a hum of noise seeping through a closed door at the other side of the room. 'Want to go through into the saloon?'

'I imagine it'll be easier to talk here,' Palmer said. 'There are a few things I wanted to clarify, Mr Hallerfield, about the death of Aaron Stein. You saw Sheriff Mitchell going to the bank that night. And you were one of the chief witnesses at his trial.'

Hallerfield grimaced.

'Sure was, though I wished I'd knowed enough to keep my mouth shut. See, that mornin' after Aaron Stein was killed, Bill Mitchell wasn't around an' folks was gettin' worried. I'd seen him go into the bank the night before, an' I thought he might have been there when the robbery took place, an' maybe he'd gotten himself hurt or somethin'. So I went to Slim Ketteridge.' He shook his bald head. 'Still don't figure Bill killed Aaron. But they got me stood up in that box at the trial an' asked me a whole heap of questions that made things look real bad for him. More I tried to make it sound better the worse it got.'

'But you have no idea who else might have robbed the bank and killed Stein.'

'Nope.' Hallerfield drained his glass and stood up. 'I gotta get back before that fool Pedro messes up. Anythin' else I can tell you?'

'Maybe. What sort of man is Slim Ketteridge?'

Hallerfield darted a sharp glance at him.

'Smart, they say. He was only a deputy a couple of years, yet here he is replacin' Bill Mitchell. Real shame he's got an alibi, ain't it? He was with Ethan Jones that night, keepin' guard over a prisoner. You spoke to Ethan yet?'

Palmer shook his head.

Hallerfield grinned again.

'Give yourself a treat. But I hope you ain't in a hurry.' He opened the door into the saloon and the hum became a roar. 'Lookee here. That's Ethan, standin' with his back against the bar. I'll go fetch him an' you can buy him a drink too. Reckon he don't often get a glass of Mary's special.'

10

Ethan Jones was thin and pale-faced with restless eyes darting from side to side, their colourless gaze never settling long on anything. His lank hair was a dull muddy brown and he smelt of stale beer.

'Mr P-Palmer? G-G-Gus said you w-wanted to t-talk to me. I'm D-Deputy J-J-Jones.' His hand moved to the badge he wore; it looked large on the scrawny chest, like it had been loaned to a child and wasn't meant to be taken seriously.

'I'm writing about the murder of Aaron Stein,' Palmer said, tossing more coins in the jar and pouring Jones a generous measure of whiskey. 'I wondered if there was anything you could tell me that didn't come up at Mitchell's trial. You fetched food from the hotel for five people that night: the sheriff, the prisoner, the two deputies and yourself. Is that right?'

'Y-yes. It w-was j-just like any other n-n-night. I d-don't recall anything s-s-special about it.' Ethan Jones drank his whiskey like he talked, in quick nervous gulps, spilling a few drops on the floor.

'And you didn't leave the jail again that night, because you and Ketteridge had a prisoner to guard.'

'That's r-right. S-S-Spurs Osgood. We w-was w-waiting for the m-m-marshal from Denver to c-come fetch him.'

Palmer topped up his glass.

'It sounds as if you were doing a deputy's job, even though you didn't have a badge.'

'I w-w-worked for Sheriff M-Mitchell nearly t-t-ten years.' Jones wasn't too steady on his feet and Palmer guided him into a chair.

'He knew you very well, but he never gave you the recognition you deserved,' Palmer suggested. 'It took Sheriff

Ketteridge to put that right. He must be a good man; it didn't take him long to figure out it was Mitchell who robbed the bank and killed Stein.'

'R-right. G-g-good man.' Jones echoed, his breathing suddenly laboured and noisy. 'M-Mitchell n-never g-g-gave me a chance. N-n-not like Slim.' His head dropped on to the table and he began to snore.

Palmer prodded him with a finger. The man snorted but didn't move. Draining his own glass Palmer pushed back from the table and left.

★ ★ ★

There were several horses tied up outside the blacksmith's shop and Palmer couldn't find room for the pinto. He led the horse in through the open double-doors, where a huge man was striking at a red-hot shoe while another who matched him in size worked the bellows at the forge. The man with the hammer spoke without pausing in his rhythmical stroke.

'You want your horse shod you'll have to wait your turn.'

'The horse is from the Lazy T. Man called Buck asked me to leave him here.' Palmer said.

The man looked up briefly.

'We heard you was coming. There's an empty stall out back. Feed in the bin if he needs it. Buck left something for you.' He jerked his head towards a shape in the corner behind the door. Palmer recognized the bag he'd carried off the train; it seemed like half a lifetime ago.

'Thank you.'

During the whole exchange the second man hadn't moved, he went on staring at the flames in the forge, his big feet spread wide for balance, a dew of sweat on his broad face.

Palmer found the stable and tended the horse. As he fetched the animal some grain he heard a step behind him. The man who'd been working the bellows stood in the doorway; there was something unnerving about the way he stared at a spot just a little to the side of where Palmer was standing. As Palmer tipped the grain into the feed-trough the big man blinked and tilted his head as if to catch the sound.

'Hello Billy,' he said.

Drawing in a quick breath Palmer hesitated a moment before he replied.

'My name's William Palmer.'

Little Pete smiled. 'I heard. You work for some newspaper back East and you dress like a dude. Talk like one too. But that's Billy Mitchell's voice, and you walk the way Billy used to walk. When a man can't see he gets to hear real good.'

'You're mistaking me for somebody else.' Palmer turned to leave but found his path barred by a bow-legged old man, a smile on the lined and leathery face beneath a battered grey Stetson.

'Unlike Little Pete I ain't blind,' Nat Grimes said. 'I had you spotted ten minutes after you got off that train yesterday, son, but I figured you didn't want nobody to know you was back. It's real good to see you, though you're kinda late. It ain't gonna be easy diggin' your pa outa this mess.'

'Quentin Jefferson was on the midday,' Little Pete said. 'Could be he's got news.'

Nat Grimes snorted.

'There ain't gonna be no reprieve, the law's the law.' He turned back to look at Palmer. 'You come up with anythin' yet, son?'

'You've got the wrong idea.' Palmer's voice was cold and remote, his eyes distant. 'I didn't come here to get the verdict changed.'

Little Pete's brow furrowed.

'You didn't?'

'What happened to you?' Palmer asked, turning away from Grimes's puzzled stare to study his old friend's face.

'Got kicked by a horse. Three years ago now, just after me and Rose got married. Doc said maybe my sight would come back but it ain't yet. I got used to it.'

Palmer suppressed a shudder, remembering his nightmare.

'Didn't you think it was strange nobody else recognized me?'

Little Pete turned his head towards the deputy.

'Well, Nat? He can't have changed that much.'

Grimes sighed. 'He's changed. An' not just on the outside. The Billy I knew wouldn't stand back and watch an innocent man hang, even his worst enemy.'

'Billy died years ago,' Palmer said coldly. 'Maybe the folk in Serenity never knew their sheriff the way he did.'

Nat shook his head.

'That ain't so. I don't know what happened the day you left, son, but it sure changed your pa. It was like a light went out inside of him. I never seed him lose his temper since that day, not once. He sure loved you, boy.'

'Then he had a strange way of showing it.' Palmer's hand lifted halfway to his scarred face then dropped.

He made to walk away but Grimes grabbed him by the arm.

'Bill had me an' Mike combin' the riverbank for days after you'd gone.'

'That's so,' Little Pete affirmed. 'Me and Jake rode out too, along with half the Lazy T crew. Sheriff Mitchell never slept the whole time. It was three days before that little mare of your ma's turned up, its neck and shoulder all covered in your blood.'

'It was like he was haunted,' Nat said. 'Tell the truth I don't think Bill ever stopped lookin' for you, not in all these years. Figure he thought findin' your dry bones'd be better'n nothin'.'

'It makes no difference now.' Palmer said. 'We're talking about Stein's death, not Billy's. The sheriff was at the bank that night. I've been questioning the witnesses and all the evidence points at him, there's no other suspect.'

'Slim Ketteridge didn't look too hard.' Nat was scornful. 'Would you condemn a man on Rufe Corder's say so?'

'Corder wasn't alone in that alleyway. Daisy Salmon heard and saw exactly the same as he did.'

'Did she?' Little Pete's sightless eyes probed Palmer's soul. 'There was something in her voice at the trial, like she knew she was doing wrong.'

'Hallerfield saw the sheriff too,' Palmer said doubtfully.

'He saw a man in a wide-brimmed hat.' Little Pete gave a slight smile. 'Sure wish I'd been in the street that night. I recall years ago seein' Ethan Jones wearin' a hat just like the sheriff's; must've been around the time you left, Billy. He only wore it once, guess he looked in the mirror and realized he couldn't fill it.'

'Ethan's one man who's in the clear,' Palmer said. 'Nobody could mistake that voice.'

'No, but there's others could sound pretty much like your pa if they wanted.' Nat said. 'Hell, it was only a couple words.'

'You won't have seen the Jeffersons

yet,' Little Pete said. 'Remember how Jake could copy your pa's voice? Used to get you jumpy as a bean. Jake wanted to stand up in court and show how easy it was to fake it but they wouldn't let him.'

'Nothing you say changes anything,' Palmer said.

Nat shook his head slowly.

'You really tellin' me you're goin' out there tomorrow to watch 'em hang your father, boy? If that's so then you're right. Billy Mitchell died a long time ago.' He spat into the dust and walked away.

★ ★ ★

Daisy Salmon came to the rendezvous with a shawl draped demurely over her bright hair but it was chosen to match her eyes, and it didn't disturb the careful arrangement of the curls that framed her face. Palmer had shaved and changed, and apart from the darkening bruises on his face he looked not unlike the Easterner who'd stepped off the train the day before. She studied his appearance with approval as he took her hand and bent to touch it with his lips.

'Miss Daisy. Forgive me, but there are things I couldn't say in front of your sister.'

She nodded in understanding and spoke confidingly.

'Violet doesn't know I'm here. I said I was going to bed with a headache.'

'It's very kind of you. I don't often get to spend time with such a pretty girl.'

Her eyes sparkled.

'Mr Palmer, you flatterer. I see so few real gentlemen here. It must be quite different where you come from.'

'Not so very different,' he said. 'There are good and bad, those who tell the truth and those who don't. You can't identify a lady or a gentleman by their clothes. Did you tell me the truth this afternoon, Miss Daisy?'

Her face flushed.

'I hope you don't think I'm a liar,' she said.

'Maybe you didn't tell lies in the witness box, but it seems to me you're hiding something.' She took half a step away but he hadn't let go of her hand. 'I need to know what really happened that night.'

'I don't know what you mean,' she said sulkily.

'Yes you do.' When she didn't answer Palmer took hold of her chin and lifted it. 'You won't have seen a hanging,' he said, drawing a finger lightly across her throat. 'It's no sight for a lady. Do you want me to tell you what it's like? It's supposed to be a quick death, but I saw a man take half an hour to die once, you wouldn't want that to happen to Bill Mitchell, would you? Especially if he's innocent.'

'But he isn't.' She pulled free from his grasp and turned away. 'What Rufe did makes no difference. The sheriff was there. He killed Mr Stein.'

'What did Rufe do?' He went after

her. 'Is he worth lying for? He ruined your chances with Jake Jefferson, but he doesn't want you, does he? He's found himself another girl.'

She stopped and glared up at him.

'What's it to you? Why do you care?'

'I thought you might have recognized me, Daisy. But then hardly anyone has. They see the scar, not the face behind it.' He looked down at her, a twisted smile on his lips.

'*Billy*. You're Billy,' she whispered. Suddenly there were tears in her eyes. 'It's too late,' she said, 'you can't save him now.'

11

Ethan Jones was still draped over the table in the little room at the rear of the Golden Gate saloon, but the whiskey bottle was empty and the lamp that hung from the ceiling had been lit, bathing the scrawny figure in a red glow.

Nobody saw Palmer go in; the woman was gone from her place at the sink, the heaps of dirty glasses spilling on to the floor. He hesitated, watching the man's back rise and fall. The noise from the saloon had swollen till it sounded like a riot; nobody would hear them leave. Grunting with the effort he lifted the unconscious man on to his back and returned the way he'd come, turning past the heaps of trash to avoid the livery yard and picking his way precariously by moonlight into a dusty wasteland beyond.

Nearly twenty years had passed since Serenity's brief spell as a boom town. A man called Wildcat Styles had uncovered a rich silver-lode no more than a mile from Main Street. Silver didn't have the same pull as gold but nevertheless men came to dig; they lived in tents, in wagons or under them, a few built cabins of wood and rubble stone. Within six months the lode was played out, and they never found another. Serenity shrank back to its former size leaving time and the wind-driven dust to cover the ruins, though here and there on the outskirts of town the remains of a shack still stood.

Palmer carried Jones to the highest standing wall, drawn by the rusty pump that stood over a patch of damp earth. A couple of ragged children came to stare, appearing out of nowhere and running when Palmer turned to face them.

The pump delivered a sluggish stream of brown water. With his head held under the flow Ethan Jones spluttered and came round, pulling free from Palmer's grip to flounder in the mud.

'You g-g-got no right . . . I'm a d-d-deputy . . . '

'Of course you are,' Palmer said, stepping back a pace to lean against the broken wall. 'Everyone knows Ethan Jones is a man of the law. An honest and upright citizen such yourself has nothing to fear if Sheriff Mitchell walks free tomorrow.'

'W-What?' There was naked terror in the colourless eyes. 'F-f-free?'

Palmer felt a chill run through him. The truth was here, but he was no longer sure he wanted to hear it.

'Nobody's going to know it was your hat the murderer wore, are they, Ethan?'

'N-n-no! I s-swear . . . I d-didn't know w-what he was g-g-going to do . . . Then it was t-too late . . . ' The words trailed into silence.

It had been a fluke shot. Palmer

stared at the sodden figure before him. He'd sought to rid himself of that last irritating shard of doubt, but Jones had just declared Bill Mitchell innocent. Serenity's sheriff hadn't robbed the bank. He hadn't killed Aaron Stein. Which meant the story of the poisoned food was true, and that led Palmer straight back to the apology for a man cowering at his feet.

'You're deep in this mess, Ethan. You fetched the meals that night. Nobody else could have made sure the sheriff got the right one.'

Jones said nothing. He lifted shaking hands to his mouth and plucked at his lips as if to enforce their silence. Palmer got to his feet and walked towards him.

'Who persuaded you to set Bill Mitchell up so they could rob the bank?'

'He d-d-deserved it!' The man rubbed mud off the badge on his vest. 'He n-n-never t-trusted me.'

'You mean he never gave you that bit of tin to wear,' Palmer said disgustedly.

'You've got a short memory. You've forgotten nobody else in this town would give you a job. Even the Corder boys stopped bullying you once the sheriff took you on. Remember that?'

'Who t-told you that?' Jones scrambled unsteadily to his feet.

'Nobody. I was there.' Palmer whipped around as a sudden burst of laughter erupted from the saloon, followed by the sound of glass shattering. Serenity was having a rowdy night. He stepped closer, turning his head so the unscarred side of his face was caught by the moonlight. 'Know who I am now?'

The slack mouth dropped open. 'You're B-B-Billy . . . '

'Yes. You'll recall I was always free with my fists, Ethan. I never had much respect for the law. I'm going to get the truth out of you if it takes me till dawn. We won't be disturbed here. Nobody's going to hear a thing.'

The terror resurfaced in Jones's pale eyes.

'N-n-no . . . '

A rifle shot rent the night. Ethan Jones tipped forward as if the drink had overcome him again, a small dark stain blossoming on his chest as he fell. Palmer reached out to catch him, letting the man's weight carry the two of them down together, rolling to bring them both into the sparse cover of the broken wall.

'Who, Ethan? Tell me,' he said urgently, as a second shot struck the wall above their heads, sending splinters of stone spitting into the night.

Ethan Jones's long thin fingers reached and clasped the badge he wore and his mouth tried to frame a word. But the fear in his eyes was gradually replaced by a detached puzzlement. Palmer hunched up on his elbows to bring his ear close to the man's lips, but it was too late; there was nothing to hear but the faint rattle of a last expiring breath.

Ducking back down Palmer felt the third shot fan his cheek. He crunched painfully into the wall and squeezed himself flat where Jones's body would shield him. Somewhere among those deserted shacks the man who'd killed Ethan Jones was intending to finish the job by silencing him as well.

As he lay low Palmer realized how much trouble he was in. The killer was good with a gun. The nearest cover was thirty yards away; few men could have made such a shot even in daylight. One of the gunslingers Red Corder had imported for his fight with the Lazy T perhaps? But that breed followed their own code of conduct, they didn't usually skulk in the dark and shoot men in the back. And the Corders were unlikely bank-robbers; they'd willingly flout the law, but Red would scorn to put the blame for his crime on another man. Besides, neither he nor his sons had the right build to pass for the sheriff that night outside the bank.

Nobody had heard the shots; since Palmer walked out of the Golden Gate the riotous noise coming from inside was being challenged by an equal ruckus from the Ace of Spades. From somewhere down by the railroad depot there came a whole volley of shots and the shrill whoop of a Rebel yell, swiftly drowned by a drunken chorus of *Yankee Doodle*.

Palmer lay in silent isolation while the ructions in the centre of town grew ever wilder. He squirmed forward on his belly, wondering if he could reach the nearest patch of cover, a large heap of rubble overgrown with thorn. A bullet slapped into the dirt only an inch from his shoulder and he wriggled back again, feeling the sweat prickling between his shoulder-blades. Though he knew how to handle a gun he never carried one; he'd rejected that way of life six years ago, along with everything else Bill Mitchell stood for.

Pale and sightless in the moonlight, Ethan Jones's dead eyes seemed to watch him. Palmer had no wish to follow wherever it was he'd gone. Keeping low, he worked one hand under the body and located the man's holster. Jones had been pretty skinny, but it was hard to lift his dead weight enough to pull the gun free.

There was something familiar about the shape of the weapon as at last it came heavily into Palmer's hand. It was a Colt Peacemaker. So it wasn't just Bill Mitchell's hat Ethan had copied. A good gun, the Peacemaker's long barrel gave it greater accuracy than many weapons of a similar calibre, but it was no match for a rifle and Palmer had no illusions about his hope of hitting anything.

He found the safety-catch, settling the gun into his right hand, trying to get the feel of the weapon, doing his best to convince himself he had a chance of getting out of this with his skin intact. He pushed his left shoulder up against Jones's body, then heaved with all his strength. The corpse rolled over and flopped into the mud beneath the pump, then it twitched violently as a shot slammed into the dead flesh.

Palmer was already on his feet, firing wildly in the direction of the tiny pin-point of light he'd been watching for, running as he emptied chamber after chamber, angling through the scattered stones towards the safety of the town. Bullets whistled through the dark, he heard one of them thud solidly into wood while another ricocheted off stone, sending sparks flying into the night.

With his last shot fired, Palmer launched himself over the low wall along the back of the livery stables, tucking his head down to roll and coming up smoothly to his feet in the middle of the crowded yard; it had been a soft landing, but he cursed as the stench hit him. He ran, dodging between horses that rolled their eyes at him and shifted uneasily, disturbed by his sudden appearance. A moment later he emerged on to Main Street.

Palmer did his best to brush wet mud and horse-manure off his coat. He dropped the empty Peacemaker into a horse-trough and tilted Buck's hat low over his face. From among the passers-by, most of them well liquored-up, he grabbed hold of a boy who looked too young to be out on such a night and pulled him into a dark corner up against the haberdasher's store.

'Want to earn a nickel?'

'Sure.' The kid smelt of beer but he didn't look to have had much.

'Find Deputy Grimes for me. Bring him here.'

'Sure,' the boy said again, smirking as he snatched for the coin. 'He's right across the street guarding the jail.'

'I said fetch him, not tell me where he is,' Palmer said, his fist closing over the money and two dirty fingers and squeezing a little. 'Say Billy wants him.'

With a nod the kid reclaimed his hand and ran.

'You told me Billy Mitchell died.' Nat Grimes faced Palmer in the darkness under the haberdasher's awning, his tone hostile. 'Don't reckon you got

141

anythin' else to say I'd wanna hear, Mr Palmer.'

'Ethan Jones just admitted the murderer borrowed that big-brimmed hat of his, the one Little Pete mentioned.' Palmer said. 'I still say Bill Mitchell's no father of mine, but you were right about one thing. I'm not prepared to watch a man hang for a crime he didn't commit.'

Grimes stared into the dark, trying to make out the face behind the voice. 'Hell, boy, why you wastin' time? We gotta make Ethan tell us who it was!'

'That could be difficult,' Palmer said. 'He's dead.'

12

'I wouldn't risk a dime on your chances of stayin' alive till mornin',' Nat Grimes said, once he'd heard Palmer's story. 'Whoever shot Ethan's gonna be gunnin' for you.'

'Then next time I'm used for target practice we have to see who's doing the shooting,' Palmer said. 'It's a shame I lost my derby hat; it made me stand out in a crowd.'

Grimes snorted.

'If you're dead you'll be no more help than Ethan.'

'I know. But we're running out of time.' Across at the sheriff's office light spilled from the windows, illuminating the men standing guard outside. 'Could he be got out of there?'

'Quentin Jefferson's talked about it, but there's half a dozen men round the jail the whole time,' Nat said.

'Tarnation, I'd try an' break him out myself if I thought there was a chance of gettin' away with it. Listen, Billy . . . ' He broke off. A thickset figure was walking past the Golden Gate, a rifle held easy in the crook of his arm. 'There's Slim, just finishin' his rounds. He ain't short on nerve, the whole town's hollerin'.'

'I suppose he didn't hear the rifle fire,' Palmer said. A quiver started somewhere at the base of his spine; Ethan Jones and Slim Ketteridge had given each other an alibi for the night of Aaron Stein's murder, and Ethan Jones had turned out to be a two-faced liar. What might that make the new sheriff?

'I wouldn't go hurryin' to talk to Slim was I you.' Nat took hold of Palmer's sleeve and pulled him deeper into the shadows. 'He figured out why he thought he knew you and he ain't too pleased.'

'What? I never saw the man before.'

'Scar or no scar, you still look a lot like your pa, and you sound like him

144

too, once a man gets used to that fancy dude way o' talkin'. Slim reckons you're here to make trouble, maybe even plannin' to break Bill out of jail. He's figurin' to lock you up until it's all over.'

'He can't do that,' Palmer said. 'Not without a good reason.'

'You're in Douglas Country here, son, mebbe things is done different back East, but you ain't in Boston now. Slim's the law in Serenity; sure you could kick up a fuss if he locks you up, but meantime your pa will have kept his date with the rope.'

'Then I'd better stay out of Ketteridge's way.'

A bunch of cowhands, all of them full of beer and looking for some other amusement, spilled out of the Ace of Spades and meandered by. Palmer ducked off the sidewalk on to the street, head down and walking fast, keeping them between him and Ketteridge.

Nat Grimes took a swift glance in the sheriff's direction, then followed.

145

'I don't know, son,' he said. 'On second thoughts, if'n you get yourself arrested you'll be safe from the sidewinder with the rifle, an' you'd have a chance to talk to Bill. No matter what he did, he's still your pa, an' he thinks you died out on the prairie six years ago. Mebbe you oughta set things straight while you got time.'

'I doubt if he cares. But there'll be time. He's not going to hang.'

They reached the blacksmith's shop and walked round to the stalls at the rear. Buck hadn't called for the pinto, it stood in the stall where Palmer had left it.

As he led the animal out a few minutes later Palmer looked around warily. There were too many shadows that could be hiding the man with the gun, but he'd walk tall and hope.

'I'm going to the Lazy T. With luck I'll be back before daybreak,' he said, putting a hand to the saddle horn.

'You're going no place.' Sheriff Slim Ketteridge stepped out from behind a wagon, a rifle to his shoulder. 'You lift your hands real smooth and there's a bunk waiting for you in the jail, mister, but if you want to argue I'm sure Hickory Salmon can find a coffin your size.'

Palmer turned slowly.

'You're arresting me?'

'Looks that way, don't it.' Ketteridge shortened the distance between them. 'Nat, take care of that horse. Mister Billy Mitchell ain't gonna need it.'

'The name's Palmer. And I've committed no crime, you've no right to arrest me.'

Ketteridge grimaced.

'You're Bill Mitchell's son, that's enough for me.'

Nat Grimes took the rein from Palmer's hand, but he didn't move away.

'Don't figure he's doin' no harm, Slim.'

'So you decided to let him go.' Ketteridge's voice was hard. He kept his eyes on Palmer. 'Just you being here causes me a pain in the belly. So long as you're on the loose you're disturbing the peace of this town, and I got enough to worry about tonight.' He walked right up close and jerked the rifle under Palmer's chin. 'Got a problem with that?'

'No.' Palmer lifted his hands. It wasn't true; the barrel of the Remington touching his neck felt slightly warm as if it had been fired recently. He wouldn't willingly go anywhere with this man. 'There's no need to lock me up. I'm leaving town.'

'The dude don't even carry a gun,' Nat said. 'He won't be causin' trouble tomorrow.'

'I got a foolproof way of making sure of that,' Ketteridge said. 'Nobody breaks out of my jail.'

'You weren't in Serenity six years ago, Sheriff. If you had been you'd know it was Bill Mitchell who left my face looking this way,' Palmer said. 'I didn't come to save his life, I came to see the bastard hang.'

'Fine, I'll make sure you get a real good view. But meantime you'll cool your heels behind bars for the night. Nat, I told you to get rid of the horse.'

How Nat came to stumble as he pulled the pinto into motion Palmer never knew, but the old man reached out a hand to stop himself falling and grabbed Ketteridge's arm, knocking the rifle down so Palmer was no longer in his sights. If it was intentional it was a crazy thing to do, but deliberate or not, Palmer didn't waste the opportunity. He flung out a powerful right fist at Ketteridge's jaw, felt a satisfyingly solid jar run up to his shoulder and watched the sheriff spin and fall. Then he was swinging aboard the pinto and drumming his heels on the horse's flanks, riding fast down the street. There was an uncomfortable itch between his shoulder blades until he turned the corner by the railroad depot and was swallowed up by the darkness, but no bullets followed him.

The road to the Jeffersons' ranch was

out the other side of town, but he worked his way around. Ketteridge wouldn't come after him; as the sheriff said, he had enough to worry about. Palmer just hoped he wouldn't be too tough on Nat.

It was late when he came in sight of the Lazy T. He stared at the dark shapes of buildings and pulled the pinto to a halt, ignoring its snort of protest; the horse was close to home and eager for its feed. For a moment he couldn't work out what was wrong, then he realized. In all the years he'd known the Lazy T there'd always been two lanterns lit on the porch come sunset, but tonight the whole ranch was in darkness, only the hazy moon, close to setting now, gave house, barn and bunkhouse a ghostly sheen. He dismounted, leading the pinto and trying to keep to the shadows.

Nothing stirred. There was a tiny noise somewhere. A rat perhaps? Palmer was out in the open now, between house and barn. The hairs on the back of his neck stood up as if a cold breath had brushed his skin.

Whether the pinto sensed his unease, or whether it scented something that he couldn't, Palmer wasn't sure, but suddenly it danced skittishly, pulling him off balance and almost tearing the rein from his hand. At that instant something zipped over his head; he heard the crash of the shot a split second later. In front of him a slight figure materialized on the ranch-house steps, moving fast.

The moonlight gleamed briefly on metal. Palmer didn't wait to see more. He threw himself to the ground. Something kicked up the dust close by and he rolled, deafened by a volley of shots, scarcely believing they'd missed. His only hope lay in reaching cover but there was a wide expanse of moonlit ground in front of him. He pushed to his feet, scooting towards the shadows. Reason told him he was a dead man. A sound from close at hand sent him spinning around; the pinto was right behind him, snorting uneasily but evidently intent on reaching the barn.

'Hold your fire!' The shout came from the bunkhouse and the voice belonged to Buck. Heavy footsteps came running. 'You'll hit Patches. Don't shoot.'

'Get a lamp here.' Higher in tone, belonging to a younger man than Buck, it was another voice that Palmer recognized.

He came down the steps from the house, light on his feet, small and razor-thin. Nothing about him looked to have changed much in six years.

Palmer stood up warily.

'Jake?'

'It's the dude,' Buck said, gathering up the pinto's rein and running a hand over the horse's neck and shoulder. 'Of all the damn fool things to do, ridin' in here at night. I told you to leave the horse with the blacksmith. It's real lucky he didn't take a bullet.'

'I had business here, thought I'd bring him home.'

A lamp came bobbing from the

direction of the bunkhouse, more men hurrying after the one who held it.

As the light spilled across the dusty yard Jake Jefferson broke open the Winchester he held and stared at the man before him.

'If I hadn't seen this myself I wouldn't have believed it. That's quite an entrance for a man who's been dead six years.'

'It wasn't quite the reception I hoped for,' Palmer said, grinning. 'I nearly split my pants.'

'Did you say split?' Jake was laughing, his eyes bright with the spark of devilment Palmer remembered. 'We're expecting the Corders. They tried to fire our barn two nights ago.'

'You know the dude, Jake?' Buck asked, looking at them open-mouthed.

'Be careful you don't swallow that horse of yours, Buck,' Jake said. 'This is William Mitchell junior, otherwise known as Billy.'

'The sheriff's son? But he calls hisself Palmer.'

'That's the name I write under,' Palmer said. 'There was already a man called Mitchell working for the *Eastern Gazette* so I took my mother's family name.'

Jake clapped Palmer on the shoulder and led him towards the house.

'It's good to see you, Billy. Whatever you call yourself you're real welcome.' He turned back to the cowhand. 'Buck, tell whoever fired off that first shot to be sure of their target next time.'

'And tell them from me I'm glad they missed,' Palmer added, 'Next time they visit the Ace of Spades, I'm buying.'

13

'I've done all I can,' Quentin Jefferson said, handing Palmer a cup of coffee. 'The governor was no help, told me we had to abide by the law.' He sighed. 'It hurts to admit it, but there's no way to break Bill out of jail, not now Slim's put a guard round him twenty-four hours a day.'

'Shame you didn't get here earlier, Billy,' Jake said. 'A week ago we might have pulled down that back wall with a good team of horses.'

'I came to cover the story of a crooked lawman,' Palmer said. 'Not to help with a jail-break.'

'What?' Jake looked at him in disbelief.

'You mean you really thought your father killed Aaron?' Quentin growled. 'Not a soul in Serenity believes he did it.'

'He nearly killed me six years ago,' Palmer said, staring into his cup. 'Guess that made it easier.'

'Bill spent the last six years regretting what he did that day,' Quentin said heavily. 'Are you ready to stand by and watch him hang because he made a mistake?'

Palmer was silent for a moment, aware of their eyes on him. He ran a finger round the neck of his shirt to loosen the collar.

'I thought I was,' he said, 'but I guess I was wrong. I didn't realize the evidence would be full of holes.'

'Knowing about Ethan's hat might have made a difference at the trial,' Quentin said. 'But now he's dead what he said to you wouldn't hold water, it's not enough to get a retrial.'

'There's something else though.' Palmer looked at Jake. 'Something I heard from Daisy Salmon.'

Quentin scowled. 'You can't trust that young woman,' he said. 'Not after the way she behaved.' He waved down his son's attempt to break in. 'It's no good arguing, Jake, even talking to Rufe Corder was an insult to you. Meeting him alone that way was unforgivable.'

'Right or wrong, she told me Rufe wasn't with her the whole time that evening,' Palmer said. 'After the man they thought was the sheriff went into the bank Rufe walked across to look through the blinds. He'd just got back to her when they heard the shot; he refused to tell her what he saw but Daisy's sure he didn't reveal the whole truth at the trial.'

'You think he saw who was in there?'

'Saw or heard. He knows something, and he kept quiet about it. Easy enough to see why.' Palmer reached for the coffee-pot and refilled his cup. As he picked it up he noticed that his hand had transferred a smear to the outside of it, and he touched his neck again, finding the place where the warm pressure of Ketteridge's rifle had bored into his skin. His fingers came away smudged with black soot.

'He's a Corder,' Quentin said. 'Since Bill's been behind bars they've tried to burn down our barn, and they're pushing our stock away from the river. Red's wanted a chance to challenge us for years and once Bill's dead the only way we'll keep that range is by spilling blood.'

'Having the new sheriff on their side would certainly make things easier,' Palmer said. 'You know Corder's brought in hired guns? I saw four when I was out there.'

'You visited the Corder place?'

'I needed to ask Rufe some questions.'

'Why?' Jake stared at him. 'You must have known he'd give you no help. The Corders want your father dead.'

Palmer met his look.

'So did I, until I found out he didn't kill Aaron Stein.' He ran a thoughtful hand down the mangled flesh on his cheek. 'He and I still have unfinished business.'

'You had your revenge six years ago,

son,' Quentin Jefferson said. 'You'd know it if you'd watched him ride out day after day searching, going without food, without sleep. It hurt him bad, never being sure if you'd survived, thinking that temper of his had killed you. When he eventually gave you up for dead he was a changed man. I never saw him lose control of himself again.' He slammed his fist on the table. 'We can't lose him this way; there must be something we can do.'

'There is.' Palmer leant back in his chair and looked at them. 'I've got an idea.'

'It had better be a good one,' Quentin said. 'I'm too old to start running from the law, and I'm damned if I'll go to jail and give the Corders the chance to move in on my range without a fight.'

'All I need is the loan of a few of your ranch hands. They won't be doing anything illegal, though I doubt if Slim Ketteridge will be too happy.'

'Pleasing our new sheriff don't rate

high hereabouts,' Jake said, grinning. 'If you've got some action in mind then count me in.'

'All right.' Palmer explained his plan. 'If you and your boys handle it right nobody will get hurt.'

'But what about the woman?' Quentin asked.

'I was planning to go and call on my sister Kate.'

The rancher and his son exchanged glances.

'You know she got married, Billy,' Jake said.

Palmer nodded. 'I heard. I'm surprised it wasn't to you.'

'I asked and she turned me down.' Jake grimaced. 'That's what caused the trouble with Daisy, I don't think I'd got your sister out of my system.'

'Violet Salmon told me Kate and her husband took on the old McEndry place. I'll head over there at first light.'

'Violet didn't tell you who her husband is, or you wouldn't be acting so calm, Billy,' Jake said. 'Kate's married to Thaddeus Corder.'

★   ★   ★

There was brightness in the eastern sky as Palmer jogged slowly towards the old McEndry ranch, letting the horse choose its own way. He rode a black mustang that had somehow never been given the Lazy T brand; its powerful haunches suggested it would have a good turn of speed. That might be useful before the day ended.

The first rays of sun shone on the McEndry place. It seemed to have shrunk since he last saw it, but patches of unweathered wood showed where the roof had been repaired, and behind the house stood the beginnings of a timber-framed barn with a heap of uncut logs alongside. Five horses stood dozing in the corral, one of them pale gold in the dawn.

Palmer climbed down from the saddle and knocked at the door. From behind the solid wood he heard a woman's voice raised in anger.

'By all the saints in heaven, if that's him . . . ' The door was flung open. Green eyes glared at him from beneath a mass of hair glowing with the red of a banked-down fire. 'Oh.'

Palmer grinned, backing away from the heavy iron poker she held.

'Good morning.'

'I thought you were Rufe,' she said, letting the poker drop, a faint flush coming to her pale cheeks. Her voice was deep, with a warmth that had been missing on their last encounter. As he stared at her Palmer felt as if somebody had kicked him hard beneath the ribs.

'I'm looking for Kate,' he said, once he'd regained the power of speech.

'It's not a good time to come callin'.' The man who appeared behind the girl had grown a little taller and his nose had set crooked, but otherwise he hadn't changed much in six years; he was tall and raw-boned, topped with the untidy thatch of Corder red hair.

'What's your business?'

'Hello, Thaddeus,' Palmer said. 'It's been a long time.'

Thaddeus Corder stared at him for a moment, squinting against the morning sun. Then he nodded.

'Flame told me you were back, Billy. What do you want?'

'A word with my sister. And to congratulate you. If I'd known I'd have brought a wedding-present.' It was impossible to keep his eyes off the girl. Flame. No other name would do justice to her; he could sense the fire within and he couldn't help his body's response. She met his look and the flush on her face deepened before she turned away.

'Kate's got nothin' to say to you.' Thaddeus made a move as if to close the door.

'At least let her tell me that herself,' Palmer said. 'Please. If she wants me to leave I won't argue.'

The man gave him a long hard look, then a faint smile appeared on his lips.

'You look like you ain't had much of a welcome home so far.' He swung the door open wide. 'I'll go talk to Kate. Flame, give the man some breakfast.'

Palmer sat at the table and watched as the girl poured him coffee, then busied herself at the stove. Thaddeus Corder disappeared into the back room. Palmer ate, hardly noticing the food, all his senses fully occupied with the girl. When she came close she smelt of fresh air and magnolia blossom, and her skin was fair and fine as flower petals. She hardly spoke but when she did every word ran through him like raw corn-liquor. With eyes averted she kept herself busy with pots and pans, but he knew she was aware of him.

'Hello Billy.' Suddenly Kate stood in the doorway. Palmer rose to his feet. He stared at her, unable to find a word that fitted the occasion. She was big-bellied with child, holding tight to her husband's hand as if she needed support. 'I didn't want to see you, but Thaddeus persuaded me I should. Say your piece, then go.'

'Kate.' He glanced at Corder; the man's face gave nothing away. 'I'm sorry you feel that way.'

She allowed her husband to guide her to a chair and she sank down heavily.

'How am I supposed to feel? You think this sets everything straight, coming back to see your father hang? Never a word, Billy, not a message or one written line to Mom in all that time, just to let her know you were still alive. How could you do that?'

'I wrote,' he said. 'When I reached Boston. Didn't she get the letter?'

Kate shook her head, tears in her eyes.

'Do you know the last thing she said before she died? She was happy, because she believed she'd finally find out what happened to you. For her, being sure you were dead would be better than not knowing. All the while she was sick that was her one shred of comfort.'

Palmer swallowed hard.

'The letter must have been lost. I'm sorry, Kate, I swear I didn't mean to hurt her.'

'Maybe not, but that doesn't make it any better. Now you've only got a few hours to make your peace with Pop.'

He reached to take her hand. It felt small and warm, just as it had when she'd run to him for protection as a child.

'I'll try to do better than that. I'll save him if I can.'

'Left it kinda late,' Thaddeus said. 'Sun's already up an' he ain't due to see it set.'

'I know.' Palmer gestured helplessly at Kate's swollen figure. 'I was after your help, Kate, but I can see that's impossible.' Swiftly he explained the plan he'd worked out with the Jeffersons.

'I could do it,' Kate said.

'No.' Thaddeus and Palmer spoke in unison.

'I'll find another way,' Palmer went on, 'You can't get involved.'

'You could dress Jake Jefferson up in a skirt and bonnet,' Thaddeus suggested. 'That I'd surely like to see.'

Despite himself Palmer grinned.

'Me too, but it can't be a man, and I need Jake.'

'He'd make a lousy woman anyway,' Flame said. 'I'll do it.'

14

'You ready?'

Nat Grimes jumped a clear foot in the air; he'd thought the wagon beside him was empty. The heap of canvas under the seat moved slightly.

'That you, Billy? Hell, boy, you just shaved ten years off my nat'ral span. Slim's outside the office talkin' to Mike Watts. You know he's deputized Red an' his boys? Best keep your head down.' Nat stepped off the sidewalk and leant against the wagon to roll a cigarette. 'Sure wish you'd let me give Bill some warnin'.'

'No,' Palmer said shortly.

'You're the boss.' The old man blew smoke. 'Nothin' else I can do?'

'Make sure you're on the posse.'

'Sure.' He turned to walk away. 'Good luck.' He crossed the street without looking back. 'Reckon you're 'gonna need it,' he muttered.

'You say something?' Slim Ketteridge asked, watching people making for the rear of the jail. The crowd around the scaffold was already ten deep.

'Gettin' old, started talkin' to myself,' Nat replied.

'You bin doin' that for years,' Mike Watts said. 'Maybe one o'clock these days you'll say somethin' worth hearin'.'

Ketteridge made a disgusted sound.

'Either of you seen Ethan this morning?'

They shook their heads, and Mike spat into the street.

'Want me to go look for him?'

'No, we're better off without that lame brain getting under our feet,' Ketteridge said. 'We've got enough men to see Mitchell off.' He went into his office.

Watts dropped his voice.

'Never thought we'd see this, Nat. Nothin's gonna save Bill now.'

'Nothin' short of a miracle,' Nat said,

following the sheriff.

The day grew hot. The crowds swelled until the street was overflowing and men were still arriving, some of them climbing on to the roofs to get a good view. Serenity hadn't seen so many people since the silver-lode ran out.

A cordon of deputies kept a space clear round the sheriff's office and the jailhouse, warding off those who were getting rowdy. As noon approached the crowd began to get restless. A brawl broke out close to the scaffold and Red and Rufe Corder waded in with fists flying to break up the fight.

The bell in the distant church tower tolled. The yells and jeers broke off abruptly and there was a moment when the whole crowd stood silent. Sheriff Ketteridge stepped out of the office. Behind him came a grey-haired man, powerfully built and with wide shoulders pulled forward by the shackles around his wrists. He was flanked by two of Red Corder's hired gunmen, while Nat Grimes and Mike Watts brought up the rear. All the guards were armed with repeating rifles and walked with their eyes on the crowd, ready for trouble.

The waiting mass of people roared. There were cries of 'shame!' from small clusters of townsfolk, soon drowned by a primeval bellow of anticipation. The mob had come to watch a man get his neck broken, though they'd have preferred a lynching; the victim died faster with a professional hangman in charge of the rope.

There were scuffles as the procession passed, but the lawmen kept moving, intent on reaching the wooden platform. Rollo Corder stood beside the dangling noose; a large imposing figure with his thatch of red hair. He had a rifle in his left hand, while the right was tucked into the front of his vest. Alongside him was the man sent by the state to perform the execution, a small portly figure dressed all in black.

Red Corder stood at the foot of the

steps looking sombre, scanning the crowd as if he expected trouble, but beside him Rufe was grinning widely. Next to them stood the parson, ready to follow the condemned man on to the platform and keep him company with a prayer during his last moments.

Few men saw the flag being raised to flutter from the top of Miss Martha Hargreave's Millinery, or noticed the man with the scarred face who swung down from the roof a moment later. He eased through the edge of the throng, heading for the old barn; a gap alongside the building gave a fleeting view of open prairie beyond. His approach was watched by a horse tied there, a black who looked as if he'd got a lot of running in him.

Further down the street, where the crowd thinned, there were four horses tethered to the back porch of the barber's shop and a clutch of cowboys lounging under the awning, their attention fixed on the railroad depot down at the southern edge of town.

Bill Mitchell walked behind Ketteridge, seeming unconcerned, apparently unaware that the mob was yelling for his blood. When he heard a friendly voice he'd turn his head and nod a greeting, but for the most part he kept his eyes fixed on the sheriff's back as they moved inexorably towards the gallows, tall above the bobbing heads, the sawn wood white against the midday blue of the sky. He knew every beam; from the window of his cell he'd watched the structure grow day by day. The uproar from the crowd rose to a crescendo.

For a whole minute the new sound wasn't heard. Deep beneath the pitch of frenzied human voices a low rumble was echoing across town, the noise throbbing up through the soles of several hundred pairs of boots. A man standing on the roof of the ten-cent diner was the first to raise the alarm. He shouted wildly and pointed towards the rail depot. Around him people followed his lead, staring south. Gradually the yells and catcalls faltered, the heads of several hundred onlookers turning as one to seek out the source of the thunder.

It grew louder, closer. The clamour of voices dropped away to nothing. Eventually the whole gathering held its breath, listening. It sounded as if a dozen railroad locomotives had abandoned the tracks down at the depot. A huge cloud of dust was advancing over the whole southern end of the town, swelling as it came and rolling skyward. Then the first bellows of the approaching cattle became audible.

A solitary voice rang out, pitched to carry loud and clear over the silent multitude.

'Stampede!'

The reaction was instant. Like wind through corn the mob rippled as men fled. They tried to squeeze back into Main Street through gaps only wide enough for half a dozen at a time. Fights broke out. Men clambered up on to roofs already overloaded until there was no more room and those who followed were thrust back to fall into the trampling mass, those above swearing and screaming, struggling to keep their places.

'Stampede!' This time the cry rose from a hundred throats and the scurrying feet raised a cloud of dust to rival the one thrown up by the charging cattle, as men battled to escape from the narrow bounds of the street.

Slim Ketteridge held Bill Mitchell by the shoulder and stood firm, staring to the south. Already the leading beasts were visible among the roiling dust, long horns curving above a close-packed swirl of red-and-white-clad flesh, charging closer with a deadly rhythm that was frighteningly fast.

He pushed his prisoner before him. The space around the gallows was clearing as the mob pushed and shoved and screamed their way into the narrow alleyways. Only Nat Grimes and Mike Watts were still with him. Rollo Corder stood on the scaffold but the rest of the deputies had fled or been dragged away by the momentum of the crowd. Ketteridge jerked his head towards the gallows.

'Come on, we'll get up there. If we bring down the leaders the rest might go around.'

A high-pitched scream rang clear above the thunder of hoofs and the bellows of the racing cattle. A wagon pulled by a pair of bay horses came round the corner on a two-wheel drift. The woman on the seat dragged frantically at the reins, barely keeping her place as the other wheels slapped back on to the ground. Eyes white with terror, necks stretched and flecked with sweat, the team was bolting, intent on outrunning the stampede.

As the rig swept by the barber's shop the four men who'd been posted there leapt from the veranda and on to their horses, riding hard and fast to swoop around and race alongside the cattle, whooping wildly and firing into the air to turn the leading steers.

Caught with a couple of yards still to

cover before he reached the safety of the gallows Sheriff Ketteridge hesitated; the wagon was heading straight for him. Then something hit him hard in the centre of his back and he fell, taking Mitchell down with him. He threw up his hands to protect his head but a boot thudded against his temple and the day split apart.

Rollo Corder had his rifle to his shoulder. He'd been waiting for this day a long time, and he wasn't going to be cheated out of seeing Bill Mitchell die. Sweeping his sights over the huddle of men on the ground he moved across Nat Grimes's scrawny back before he let out a long steadying breath. Bill Mitchell was half-way to his feet, one hand on the ground, unaware that he was about to keep his appointment with death.

A bullet was just as sure as a rope. Rollo took aim with care, leaning against the gallows to hold him steady.

'So long, Sheriff,' he said, and squeezed the trigger.

Jerking back as the recoil smacked into his shoulder Rollo didn't see Mitchell fall; his eyes were drawn to the wagon hurtling towards the scaffold. Behind it came a black horse ridden hard, heading straight for the lawmen. Rollo grunted to himself; the stampede was no accident, the Jeffersons had planned a rescue. He straightened swiftly, easily working the under-lever Winchester with the weakened spring one-handed and taking aim at the man on the black; any bastard who tried to help Mitchell was asking for trouble.

The horse swerved suddenly and Rollo swore as his shot went wide. The rider was still coming, though, and he panned round to try again. His gaze fell on the woman, standing in the wagon now and wrestling with the reins. Flame was laughing, intoxicated by the speed and danger as she fought the powerful horses. She had her head thrown back, red hair streaming in the wind.

Rollo forgot about the rider. The girl was a Corder. That made the betrayal that much worse. *Treacherous bitch!* Rollo's finger tightened on the trigger, a smile on his lips as he gave it that last fatal squeeze.

Flame slipped down on to the seat, a shudder passing through her. She had the team back under control and the wagon was slowing, skidding past the men on the ground. Chirruping to the horses, she brought them round into a sweeping curve, passing by the barn with no more than an inch to spare and returning on the other side of the scaffold where she brought the rig to a halt beside Mitchell, now on his hands and knees.

Palmer drove the black towards the gallows, intent on reaching Rollo. Suddenly a man stood up from beneath the scaffold; he must have been knocked down in the rush but now he was on his feet again, a man with faded red hair holding a long-barrelled Winchester in his hands. Red Corder fired, and Palmer's horse staggered on for a couple of paces before its legs gave way and it somersaulted, throwing him over its head. He rolled, letting the impetus of the fall carry him to the foot of the scaffold where he came upright to slam Red Corder back against the beam of wood, one hand swiping the rifle away, the other landing squarely on the man's jaw.

Before Corder landed unconscious on the ground Palmer was moving towards the ladder. He was on it, racing up two steps at a time when the sharp report of a rifle echoed along the street. He reached the platform to see blood spurting spectacularly from a hole in Rollo Corder's neck. The rifle fell from the man's nerveless hand and he pitched forward off the platform to thud down beside his father.

As he leapt back to the ground Palmer came face to face with Mike Watts. The deputy stood beside Bill Mitchell. Serenity's one-time sheriff had his manacled hands pressed to the spreading patch of blood high up on his chest.

'Guess I've had my fill of bein' a lawman,' Watts said. He bent over Slim Ketteridge, who didn't stir as Watts removed a key from his pocket. The deputy unlocked the handcuffs. 'I quit.'

Between them Watts and Palmer hoisted Mitchell into the back of the wagon. Nat Grimes lay apparently unconscious on the ground, but as Palmer ran around to jump up beside the girl he saw his old friend wink broadly.

Flame whipped up the horses and the wagon rocked and swayed, sending up plumes of dust from the wheels as they skidded through the narrow gap beside the barn and out on to the open prairie. A few wild shots kicked up dirt and shouts of fury followed them.

It seemed folk were angry at the loss of the day's entertainment.

15

Men were trickling back from Main Street and climbing down from the roofs. The cattle were no more than a cloud of dust and a low rumble of sound as they disappeared across the open prairie. Rufe Corder pushed himself up from the sidewalk by the jail, an angry swelling on his cheek and his vest torn half off his back. Two men stood in his way and he shouldered them roughly aside.

It looked as if a battle had been fought beneath the gallows. Red knelt by the body of his eldest son; Rollo lay beneath the scaffold gazing sightlessly at the sky, a wide pool of blood soaking into the dust beneath him.

'You see who did it?' Rufe asked.

'No. He was hidin' out there behind the barn, but I'd stake a thousand dollars to a bent nickel he was from the

Lazy T.' Red leant over to close Rollo's eyes, a cold fire burning in his own. 'It's time we dealt with the Jeffersons.'

'That girl on the wagon. It looked like Flame.' Rufe stared past the barn but he could see nothing but a great cloud of dust.

'It was. An' if she's taken up with those murderin' bastards I swear she's no kin of mine. When we've put Quentin an' his whelp underground where they belong we'll teach her a thing or two.'

'That's for me to do, Pa. Once she's wed to me I'll learn her real good. What happened to Mitchell?'

'Ain't he here?' Red looked around. 'I thought Rollo got him before he shot the girl.'

Slim Ketteridge and Nat Grimes were both stirring, not far from the body of a black horse.

'You see where Mitchell went, Sheriff?' Red asked.

'Didn't see a thing,' Ketteridge said, wiping a trickle of blood from the cut above his ear.

'Must've been on that wagon,' Rufe said.

Ketteridge nodded.

'Along with that lying two-faced son of his.'

'Son?' Red Corder stared at him. 'Bill Mitchell's boy died years ago. Rumour was he killed the boy hisself.'

'Guess that scar threw you. He's the dude from the *Eastern Gazette*.'

'Palmer!' Rufe said. 'I thought there was somethin' familiar about him. So Billy Mitchell ain't dead.'

'Looks that way,' his father said. 'Reckon we'll put that right. Go find Hickory, son, tell him to see to your brother. Then fetch our horses. We got things to do.'

'No.' Slim Ketteridge picked up his Winchester and worked the action, checking it was clear of dust. 'You're deputies. You'll wait and ride with the posse.'

'Somebody just killed my son,' Red roared. 'I ain't waitin' for no posse. You don't tell me what to do, Ketteridge, not unless you want — '

'Shut your noise!' The sheriff lifted the rifle, snapping a round into the breech. 'This is my town, Corder, and don't you forget it.' He lowered his voice. 'Half the town saw Rollo take a shot at the girl.' He jerked his head towards the men around them. 'Reckon they'd say the man who killed Rollo was protecting her.'

'She was helpin' Mitchell cheat the rope,' Rufe protested.

'And we'll deal with her along with the rest of 'em,' Ketteridge said, 'but it has to be done right.'

Red Corder's reply was a hoarse whisper, but his eyes were hard chips of steel and his face was flushed darker red than his hair.

'Just remember me an' my boy can bring you down any time we choose, *Sheriff*. We're finishin' Mitchell an' the Jeffersons, with or without you. As for the girl, she's our business; the Corders take care of their own.' He glanced at

Rufe, aiming the words at his son as much as Ketteridge. 'The boy here gets her, soon as we've settled with the Lazy T.'

'All right.' Ketteridge raised his voice, staring at the growing crowd. 'I want all those who were deputized to report to my office right now, along with anyone willing to join the posse.'

★　★　★

The wagon bounced, its springs creaking. After a short spell on the road they'd turned off it and Palmer was trying to pick a level route across a waste of split rock.

'You'll kill him if you keep on this way.' Flame sat on the wooden boards with Bill Mitchell's head on her lap, pressing her hand against the wound in his chest. He'd passed out only minutes after they left Serenity. 'We need to stop so I can take care of this.'

'We don't have time,' Palmer said, coaxing the flagging horses. 'The posse must be after us by now, and if they catch us they'll hang him from the nearest tree. If we can't get him to the border we'll have to find a place to hide.' Glancing back he saw a lone horseman racing across the prairie towards them, a billowing cloud of dust filling the sky behind. He tensed, slapping the reins on the horses' backs, a hand reaching for the whip.

'It's all right,' Flame said. 'That's no posse.'

Jake Jefferson slowed his horse to an easy lope beside the wagon.

'The boys'll drive the herd back to the depot,' he said. 'They did a pretty good job of wiping out your tracks.'

'You two weren't supposed to get involved,' Palmer said.

'What were you going to do? Pick Mitchell up and carry him half-way across the state on your back?' the girl asked acidly. 'Once you lost your horse the wagon was the only way to get him out of there.'

'And I don't see why you're mad at

me,' Jake said, 'Rollo was getting ready for another shot. Or maybe since they're kin you figure it didn't matter if he put another bullet in her . . . '

Palmer slammed his foot on the brake and heaved on the lines. As the wagon slewed to a halt he turned to look at Flame. The left sleeve of her dark green dress was stained from just below the shoulder down to the wrist. 'He hit you?' he said disbelievingly, touching the sticky stain with one finger.

'It's nothing,' she said. 'Just a graze. Keep going. We have to get the sheriff under cover so I can tend him properly.'

'Be better if you patch him up so he can ride,' Jake said.

'I've told you, he's in no state to ride in a wagon, let alone on a horse.'

Jake frowned.

'Maybe you're not too bothered if Red and Rufe catch up to us.'

Flame glared at him.

'Rollo shot me. If I wasn't on your side before I sure as sugar am now. But

I suppose no Jefferson's ever going to trust a Corder.'

'You got your family's way of seeing things, sure enough,' Jake said. 'Next time I won't bother saving your life.'

'Shut up, Jake.' Palmer whipped the horses back into motion. 'I'd be grateful if you'd both stop arguing and help me decide where we're going before that posse arrives.'

★ ★ ★

Quentin Jefferson stared at the array of weapons laid out on his desk. There were two old Enfield muzzle-loaders, relics from the war. After that things improved a little; there was a Henry and two Winchesters with plenty of ammunition. He picked up the newest Winchester and loaded it, pleased to find his hands were steady.

Buck came to the door, screwing his battered face into a grin.

'Cattle are safe in the pens at the depot, boss. I left Shorty an' Cal to keep an eye on 'em till they're loaded tonight.' He shifted his weight from one foot to the other. 'The boys said to tell you we're right behind you. Say the word an' I swear we won't let nobody search this place, not unless they bring the army with 'em, an' even then we'd give 'em a fight.'

The rancher smiled.

'Let's hope it doesn't come to that. Slim Ketteridge may be no friend to the Lazy T but he's always stood by the rule of law.'

'Riders comin'!' The shout took them to the door. Out across the plain a group of horsemen approached, sending a great plume of dust into the air as they came.

'What was that you said about an army?' Jefferson said. 'Looks like Slim's near enough emptied the town.'

'We're ready for 'em,' Buck said. Dawson came from the bunkhouse and tossed him a rifle. 'If we put a couple of men on the roof an' share the rest between the barn an' the bunkhouse —'

'No.' Quentin Jefferson stared at the dust cloud. It was impossible to count the riders but there had to be twenty at least, and with two of his hands in town and Jake missing he had only eleven men. 'I'll talk to the sheriff. You boys just keep an eye on the Corders and their hired guns but don't any of you get itchy fingers.'

Ketteridge rode at the head of the posse, with Nat Grimes and Judge Winterson on one side and the Corders on the other. Half a dozen of Red's hired hands followed close behind, then a clutch of townsmen, among them Hickory Salmon, Big Pete and Gus Hallerfield.

'Mr Jefferson.' Ketteridge nodded a greeting as he pulled up. 'You'll know why we're here. We're looking for a couple of murderers.' He glanced at Buck and the other cowboys standing tense and ready behind the rancher, all of them with rifles in their hands. 'Seems too much of a coincidence, your cattle stampeding into town like that.

Reckon I'd be within my rights if I took you in for helping Mitchell escape.'

'It was an accident, Sheriff. Buck here can tell you what happened.'

'Sure thing. We had the steers headin' for the pens at the depot,' Buck said. 'The train started hissin' an' puffin' an' them cattle got kinda spooked, then the dam' fool engineer blowed the whistle. Guess that was more'n they could stand, them steers turned and lit out like their tails was on fire.'

'It's lucky my boys managed to turn the herd before they got loose in town,' Quentin said. 'Somebody could have got hurt. I'm real glad they didn't.'

Ketteridge nodded slowly, eyeing the cowhands.

'Fact remains, your friend Mitchell got loose. I'm gonna have to ask you to let my men search your place.' He glanced at Winterson. 'I brought the judge along, just to make sure everything's done fair an' legal.'

Winterson kneed his horse a little closer.

'It doesn't look good, Quentin,' he said. 'Rollo Corder's dead. Witnesses seem to think Jake fired the shot. It's the sheriff's duty to search for him, as well as Bill Mitchell.'

'Stop pussyfootin' around,' Red Corder growled. 'Jefferson's been shootin' his mouth off ever since Stein was murdered.' He glared at the rancher. 'Your son killed my boy while he was breakin' Mitchell free, Jefferson. We've come for the pair of 'em.'

'Shut your mouth, Red,' Ketteridge said, stepping down from the saddle. 'Well, Mr Jefferson? Do we take a look inside?'

'I'm not having any Corder in my house, nor any of that trash they brought with them,' Jefferson said. 'But you and my neighbours from Serenity are welcome, Sheriff. I have nothing to hide.' He stepped aside to let Ketteridge and Judge Winterson lead half a dozen men into the house, but he kept the loaded rifle in his hands, his eyes on Red Corder.

'Reckon it ain't too late to stretch Mitchell's neck before the sun goes down, an' that scaffold's got room for two.' Red Corder said. 'Where's that brat of yours, Jefferson? Had to be him hidin' out at the barn. He never had the guts to take my boys on out in the open.'

Buck growled something and moved closer, flanked by the rest of the Lazy T hands.

'Take it easy,' Quentin said. 'I'll not let a loud-mouthed hot-head rile me. Seems maybe I should say I'm sorry about your son, Red, but I never could abide a liar. Truth is, he was damn lucky Bill didn't kill him six years ago when he tried to murder Jake.'

'You shut up about my brother,' Rufe said, spurring his horse forward. 'You ain't the big man around here no more Jefferson. There's no tame sheriff runnin' at your heels now.'

'That's enough.' Nat Grimes pushed his horse between the two of them, his Navy Colt in his hand. 'Red, you tell your boy to back off or so help me you'll be buryin' him alongside Rollo.'

'Quiet down the lot of you,' Ketteridge said, coming out of the house and directing his deputies to search the other buildings. When they reappeared shaking their heads he remounted, edging his horse close to the rancher. 'There'll be deputies keeping an eye on this place, Jefferson, and if Mitchell comes here you'd best hand him over, unless you want to spend a few years in the state pen. As for Jake, you can tell him from me, if he gives himself up I'll see he gets a fair trial.'

Quentin Jefferson snorted.

'Sure, as fair as Bill's.'

Ketteridge nodded.

'That's right, Jefferson. You tell him, Winterson.'

The judge looked unhappy but he gave a curt nod.

'The law's the law, Quentin. You'd best learn to accept it.'

As the posse rode away Red Corder turned and headed back, reining in beside the rancher and glowering down at him.

'I don't give a cuss about the law, Jefferson. The Lazy T's finished, an' you an' your son along with it.'

16

Compared with the Lazy T the old McEndry ranch looked like a shack in the middle of a wasteland. Fifty head of cattle grazed on either side of a wide arroyo while four horses stood dozing in a small corral. One of them was a palomino.

Ketteridge took only the two Corders with him, leaving the rest of the riders by the fallen gateposts which had once supported McEndry's sign. Thaddeus Corder stood in the doorway as they rode up, his arms folded across his chest. He nodded briefly to his father and brother then turned to the lawman.

'What's your business here, Sheriff?'

'We're looking for Flame Corder,' Ketteridge said. 'Heard she was staying with you and your wife.'

'Powerful lot of men to seek out one woman,' Thaddeus remarked. 'Ain't seen her since this mornin'. She went into town.'

'The bitch helped Bill Mitchell escape,' Red Corder said. 'An' the Jefferson brat shot Rollo.'

Thaddeus's head jerked up.

'Yeah, he's dead,' Rufe put in. 'You see what you done, Thad, takin' up with the Mitchells. You never should've married that — '

'You leave my wife out of this.' His voice was cold. 'Flame ain't here.'

'We've got no quarrel with you, but I figure the girl might lead us to Mitchell,' Ketteridge said. 'He's the one we're after.'

'He ain't here either.' Thaddeus turned and beckoned to somebody inside the cabin. Kate Corder stepped out, her hands held protectively over her swollen belly. 'Go take a look-see, Sheriff.'

Ketteridge was inside no more than half a minute.

'When did you last see Bill Mitchell?' he asked.

'You're upsettin' my wife, Ketteridge. We already told you, her pa ain't here.' Thaddeus waved a hand at the tiny cabin. 'Did you look up the chimney?'

The sheriff stared around, taking in the half-built barn and the ground around it, scattered with sawdust and shavings. A stack of logs was piled haphazardly alongside, waiting to be cut.

'I want all that timber moved.'

'You figure I got somebody hidin' under there?' Thaddeus went across and put a boot to the precarious heap, thrusting hard at it. The logs ground together, several of them rolling off the top and crashing to the ground. 'They just got their head stove in. Now get off my land.'

Ketteridge shrugged and put his foot in the iron.

'If the girl comes back you bring her into town,' he said, turning his horse to rejoin the rest of the posse.

'That's my horse you got there,' Rufe said, his eyes on the palomino.

'Seem to recall I broke him, little brother,' Thaddeus replied. 'You wanna fight me for it?'

'Ain't worth that; plenty more where he come from,' Red said. 'We got more serious things to talk about. Thaddeus, you must've known that girl was helpin' Mitchell. Why d'you let her do it, boy?' He jerked his head at Kate. 'She talk you into it?'

'He's gone soft in the head,' Rufe said savagely. 'He don't even care 'bout Jake killin' his brother. Where's the girl, Thad? It's time she got halter-broke.'

'You figure you're man enough for that?' Thaddeus asked. 'Flame's too much for you, Rufe. Grow up some, or get yourself some help. She won't never come to you willin'.'

Rufe flung himself off his horse.

'You sonofabitch, maybe you been beddin' her yourself, seein' your own woman's whelpin' — ' The words choked off as Red's hand grabbed hold of his neckerchief and yanked him back. He clawed at the cloth, struggling to free himself with eyes bulging from a face that was rapidly turning purple. 'Enough, Pa,' he croaked.

Red let him go. The youngster climbed sullenly back aboard his horse, rubbing his neck.

'Thaddeus, we ain't too concerned about the girl, not right now.' Red glanced at Kate, still standing by the door of the cabin, her face white. 'We want Mitchell, an' we're gonna pay the Jeffersons, with Ketteridge or without, makes no never mind to me. They murdered your brother, boy. Your own flesh an' blood. If'n you're still a Corder you'll help us. You bear that in mind now; with us or against us, there ain't no middle way.' He touched his hat to Kate and turned away.

Kate hurried to her husband's side as the two riders galloped after the rest of the posse. She motioned to the stack of timber.

'Thaddeus . . . '

'Not yet,' he said, taking her hand and steering her back to the cabin.

'There's likely somebody watchin'. Sun'll be down in an hour.'

It was pitch-dark when three shadowy figures led their horses into the corral. There was no light in the cabin, and Thaddeus walked across from the doorway to greet them.

'Where d'you leave the wagon?'

'Hidden in the bottom of the arroyo where it bends north,' Palmer said, removing the harness from the horse he was leading. 'You'd have to be close to see it. Did you get him out yet?'

'No. I was afeard of tippin' a log into the hole.'

Palmer nodded. 'Flame, you'd better get inside, let Kate bind up that arm for you.'

The girl hesitated, throwing down the bridle she'd taken off the second horse, then she pursed her lips and went into the cabin. Thaddeus gave a wry grin.

'Never seen that gal do as she was told before,' he said.

Jake Jefferson heaved his saddle on to the fence.

'Have any trouble with the posse?'

'No. But they're lookin' for you. Said you shot Rollo.'

There was a heavy silence between them.

'It was him or the girl,' Jake said at last. 'He'd already winged her. Pretty clear field of fire from up on the scaffold and he came close to killing the sheriff.'

Thaddeus nodded slowly.

'He was good with that gun. Spent whole days practising after he lost the use of his arm.

'This isn't the time to talk,' Palmer said. 'There's work to do.' Without looking back at the other two men he went across to the log-pile. Corder and Jefferson exchanged a glance that had nothing of friendship in it, then they followed. It took several minutes to reach Bill Mitchell where he lay curled up at the bottom of the sawpit. Hiding the fugitive there had been Flame's idea. She came now to help lift him out, cradling his head as they hurried him into the cabin. Thaddeus barred the door and lit a lantern.

'Put him here on the table,' Flame said. She cut away Bill Mitchell's soiled shirt and vest, stiff with dried blood; then, with deft fingers, she cleaned and probed the wound. Flame scowled down at the swollen and discoloured flesh. 'This should have been done hours ago. Kate, I need the knife you got ready for me.'

'Where did you learn to do that?' Palmer asked a few moments later, as the girl dropped the misshapen bullet on to the table.

'I'm a Corder,' she said flatly. 'My father spent his whole life on the wrong side of the law. Three times he trailed home with a bullet in him, and there were others . . . '

'Will he be all right?' Kate asked, gently cupping her hands around her father's head.

Flame put her head to the injured man's chest and listened. 'Heart's beating strong,' she said. 'Just hope the fever doesn't set in.'

'He goin' in the pit again?' Thaddeus asked. 'I reckon that posse'll be back.'

'He needs rest,' Flame cautioned. 'We can put him in my bed for a while. Surely the sheriff won't come back till morning?'

'We'd better hope not,' Palmer said grimly, 'but we need to be gone well before dawn.'

'You must all be pretty hungry,' Kate cut in swiftly. 'Thaddeus, why don't you pour everyone some coffee while I set out a meal?'

'Reckon it's time I was going,' Jake said, heading for the door.

Thaddeus stepped into his path.

'Why? Thinkin' of cuttin' yourself a deal with the law, Jefferson? Guess you won't want to face a charge of murderin' my brother.'

Jake was suddenly still, the tension visible in every muscle of his body.

'For your wife's sake I'll pretend I didn't hear that.'

'Then what's your rush?' Thaddeus

moved back to take the pot of coffee from Kate.

'I don't take hospitality from a Corder.'

'You figure we plan to poison you?' Thaddeus put the coffee-pot back on the stove so hard that it spilt, the liquid hissing as it hit the hot metal.

Flame gave an unladylike snort of derision.

'Rest of your kinfolk's out for my blood,' Jake said at last.

Kate took hold of her brother's arm.

'Billy?' she whispered.

'You just spent three hours lying across a horse's head at the bottom of a dry riverbed,' Palmer said, looking at Jake's red-rimmed eyes and filthy face. 'And you don't have the sense to accept a cup of coffee? Hell, Jake, if you're so stupid how come you and I were friends?'

Jake's eyes glittered. Then suddenly he relaxed and smiled.

'Sure, I don't know,' he said. 'Maybe I ain't as clever as you, Billy, but at least

I ain't as ugly either.'

'Jake!' Kate protested.

Thaddeus and Palmer laughed.

'He's got a point,' Palmer said.

'I don't think he's ugly,' Flame said, then she flushed deeply and was suddenly busy tending to her patient.

'From what you was sayin' earlier, you figure Slim Ketteridge had somethin' to do with that bank robbery,' Thaddeus said, pushing back his chair after they'd finished eating. 'You got any ideas about provin' it?'

Palmer shook his head.

'Daisy says Rufe went to look in through the door of the bank that night, but he never told her what he saw.'

'Red was crowing about something the next couple of days,' Flame said. 'And Rufe said they'd got Slim where they wanted him.'

'None of which gets us any further,' Palmer said. 'Hearsay won't stand up as evidence in court.' He looked at Thaddeus. 'They didn't tell you any of this?'

'Nope. They ain't exactly friendly since I married Kate. Can't help but wonder where Pa got enough money to hire them gunslingers, though.'

'You mean he's using the haul from the bank?' Jake said. 'But Rufe couldn't have killed Stein, and there's not one of 'em could be mistaken for Bill Mitchell, even on a dark night.'

'No, but suppose it was Ketteridge, and Rufe saw him,' Flame said. 'Maybe Rufe's being paid to keep his mouth shut.'

'There's one man who'd know if Ketteridge left the jail that night.' Bill Mitchell had come to the door of Flame's room. 'And I think I know where to find him.'

Palmer stiffened at the sound of the familiar voice behind him. Kate glanced at her brother, then rose to go to her father's side.

'Pop? You shouldn't be out of bed. How are you feeling?'

'Like a kitten who just lost a fight with old Beecher's barn-dog,' he said.

'If you're right about Ketteridge you need to talk to Spurs Osgood.'

Palmer pushed his chair slowly back from the table, got up and turned around. Bill Mitchell leant against the doorpost, not steady enough on his feet to walk into the room. His hair was still thick but it was almost white, and there were a lot of lines his son didn't remember around the eyes and mouth; in six years he'd aged twenty. Already drained of blood by his wound, the sheriff's face was deathly pale as he met Palmer's eyes.

'Dear God,' he whispered.

17

Fifteen horsemen gathered outside the sheriff's office at first light. Serenity was quiet, though Main Street was littered with broken bottles, and the sign outside the Golden Gate saloon was peppered with bullet holes. The sightseers and drifters filling the town had made up for the lack of entertainment the previous day. The posse rode out, backs hunched against the morning chill; a train whistled mournfully from the southern end of town.

'What you reckon to do?' Red Corder asked, spurring his horse alongside Slim Ketteridge.

'We'll visit your boy again. That wife of his looked jittery when we went visiting.'

Red snorted. 'She just ain't the friendly type. While we're wastin' time around town Mitchell could be half-way to the county line.'

Ketteridge shook his head.

'He's carrying a bullet. He won't be riding far or fast, and he can't outrun us in that wagon. Besides, where else d'you figure we go? Couldn't find no trace of a trail after Jefferson's cattle went through.'

'We could go back to the Lazy T.' Red suggested. He'd brought Rufe and four hired guns along; there were ways of forcing a man's hand. 'Jefferson was mighty accommodatin' yesterday, maybe he figures we won't be lookin' for Mitchell there again.'

'Quentin ain't fool enough to hide Mitchell at the ranch, but there's a chance that pup of his will run home to his pa. If we don't pick up some trace at the McEndry place we'll check it out.'

'Hey, look there.' Rufe Corder pointed towards the railroad depot. The Eastbound train was gathering speed, and a lone horseman was galloping after it on a mount that shone gold in

211

the light of the rising sun. 'That's my horse!' There was something unusual about the way the rider was dressed; he wore a dusty Stetson, but it didn't set right with the pale-brown coat and pants. 'It's the dude!' He dug his spurs savagely into his horse's flanks.

'Palmer!' Ketteridge spat out the single word, turning his horse after the younger man. Red was right there with them, racing his son and the sheriff as they angled to cut the rider off, the rest of the posse straggling out behind.

The man on the palomino was alongside the last car now, slowing the horse to match the speed of the train. He reached out and got a hand to the railings around the platform at the rear, kicked his feet free of the irons and swung himself up. With a swift wave to the men chasing him he disappeared into the car, and the palomino turned away, slowing to a jog as the other horses approached.

Rufe raked his mount's sides, driving it to a burst of speed that left the others behind. Red and Ketteridge hauled off, swinging away from the rails. Crouching low, Rufe reached out and for a second his finger tips brushed the rail, but the horse had no more to give and the train was pulling away.

'I'll get you, Billy,' he yelled. 'Godamn coward!' Belching smoke the iron horse roared eastwards, a last long whistle mocking Rufe's attempt to catch it. He swept round to pick up the palomino's trailing rein and rode back to rejoin the rest of the posse.

'Guess the dude's nothin' but a yellow-belly,' he said.

Red Corder spat out a mouthful of dust.

'Fancy bit of riding for a dude.'

Nat Grimes grinned, coming up alongside. He was followed by Judge Winterson, Gus Hallerfield, Big Pete the blacksmith and Hickory Salmon; Nat was doing his best to keep his word to the boy and make sure Mitchell had some friends on the posse; if the Corders and their hired guns caught up with him they'd likely string him up to the nearest tree, unless they shot him first.

'Quentin always reckoned he was one of the best hands he ever had,' Nat lied. 'Young Billy could do anythin' with a horse.'

Gus Hallerfield's lips twitched then he nodded solemnly.

'Sure thing,' he said. 'Suckled by a mare, that one.'

'Well, he ain't on a horse now,' Ketteridge said. 'And with a face like that he won't be easy to miss. Nat, you'd best ride back to town and send a telegram to Marshal Leyden at Pacetown. Have him meet the train and lock Palmer up for a few days till I can get along there an' pick him up.'

'Where'll I find you?' Nat asked.

'We're going to have another word with Mitchell's daughter. You can catch up with us at the McEndry place.'

★ ★ ★

214

Thaddeus Corder was heaving a log from the stack when the posse arrived. He strode across to intercept the horsemen as they drew up outside the cabin.

'I already told you Flame ain't here,' he said.

'Palomino's gone,' Ketteridge pointed out, nodding towards the horses in the corral.

'Went durin' the night. Figured Rufe came an' took it.' His brother sat the bright horse, leading a bay. 'Looks like I was right.'

'Weren't me,' Rufe said. 'But seein' as how you're still family I'll leave you the bay. Reckon that's fair.' He rode across and hitched the horse to the fence. 'Your friend Palmer rode this cayuse of mine to catch the Eastbound this mornin'. You sayin' you don't know nothin' about that?'

Thaddeus shrugged.

'I got better things to do at night than sit guard over the corral.'

'Like help Bill Mitchell get away?'

Ketteridge said.

'Like sleep,' Thaddeus told him. 'An' right now I'm busy, so why don't you take your damn posse an' get off my land.'

'Need to take a look inside again,' the sheriff said. 'Real sorry to disturb you.'

'My wife's pretty near her time,' Thaddeus said, moving across to block the door. 'Bad enough she's lost her pa, without you keep botherin' her.'

'But maybe her pa ain't lost,' Red Corder said, lighting down to come face to face with his son. 'Figure I'll go talk to my daughter in law, Thaddeus. After all, she's gonna make me a gran'pappy any day now. No need for anyone else to trouble the girl. Don't reckon she'll mind me visitin'.'

Reluctantly Thaddeus stood aside. Slim Ketteridge rode his horse under the framework that would one day be a barn, scanning the heaps of sawdust and the uncut logs, then he circled the cabin, staring at the ground, pulling up suddenly and pointing at a line of

216

round marks in the dirt

'That's blood,' he said.

'Mine.' Thaddeus Corder raised his left hand to show a rag tied around his thumb. 'Got careless with the saw. Hurt like hell.'

'Rider coming,' Big Pete said. 'Looks like Nat.'

Ketteridge grunted and turned to meet the deputy.

'Send that telegram?'

'Sure did,' Grimes replied.

'All right. We're wasting time.' Ketteridge gathered the posse around him. 'Fan out and see if that wagon came here. Could be more than one horse left this morning.'

Nat Grimes rode up the arroyo flanked by Gus Hallerfield and Big Pete, waving off two of Corder's hired men who made to follow. With a quick glance over his shoulder to check that nobody was watching them, Nat rode down into the dry creek to look at the abandoned wagon while Gus and Big Pete went on by, ignoring him. A moment later he rejoined them.

'Well?' Gus prompted.

'Powerful lot of blood,' Nat growled. 'Reckon Ketteridge is right. Bill ain't gonna be ridin' to the border anytime soon.'

It was Rufe Corder who found the tracks, less than half a mile from McEndry's old sign. Three horses had headed north-west, travelling fast. He summoned the rest of the posse with a couple of shots from his .45.

'We got 'em,' he yelled. 'Must be Mitchell an' Jefferson an' the girl.'

'Not more than four hours old,' the sheriff said, staring down at the scuff marks in the dirt. 'Seems like that boy of yours has been lying to us, Red.'

'I'll deal with Thaddeus when we get back,' Corder said. 'Right now we got business with Mitchell.'

Ketteridge drove the posse hard, intent on gaining ground on the fugitives before rain washed away their tracks, for the day was growing sultry, heavy storm-clouds piling over the mountains to the west. They paused for a few minutes around noon, letting the horses drink from a muddy water-hole, some of the men breaking out rations while others curbed their hunger with a cigarette or a plug of chewing tobacco.

'One thing I can't figure.' Rufe Corder threw down his cigarette butt. 'How come they ain't headin' west? County line's a whole lot closer that way, an' the country's wild. Doubt we'd be able to track 'em.'

'I was wondering the same thing,' Ketteridge said. 'But if they go west they'll hit the mountains that much sooner, and there's places a horse has to be led. If Mitchell's carrying a slug around with him he won't be wanting to walk.'

By nightfall the men and horses were sweat-streaked and covered in dust; the storm still hadn't broken and the air felt thick and stale in their mouths.

'We'll make camp,' Ketteridge announced. 'We made up some time. I'd say we're not more than an hour behind.' He scanned the leaden sky to the west; above them it was already black. 'Won't be no moon tonight unless that storm backs off and with a wounded man I don't reckon they'll risk riding in the dark. We'll post a watch in case it clears. Soon as there's light enough to travel we'll move on, so eat fast and get some sleep while you can.'

Nat Grimes eased wearily off his horse, keeping a tight hold on the horn so his knees didn't buckle. He grimaced as he struggled to undo the cinch; it had been a long time since he'd ridden a full day.

'Here, old-timer, let me give you a hand.' It was one of Corder's hired guns, the one they called Poker. 'You must be powerful desperate for that two dollars a day,' he said, lowering Nat's saddle to the ground.

'I'm a deputy,' Nat snarled. 'Been helpin' to keep the law in Douglas County since before you was born, boy, an' most of that time I rode alongside Bill Mitchell.'

Nothing changed in Poker's sallow face.

'Must be kinda strange huntin' down a man you worked for.'

'Strange ain't the word for it,' Nat replied, picking up his bedroll and turning his back.

Lightning flickered over the distant mountains and all night the thunder rolled like an endless procession of wagons through the high country, but no rain fell where the posse had set their camp and by daybreak they were in the saddle again, wisps of mist rising around the horses' feet. In the grey morning light they lost the trail for a while on a shelf of splintered rock, and Ketteridge scattered the posse to look for signs. Nat would have kept quiet about the remains of a fire tucked under the lee of an outcrop but Poker was close behind him and he found the trampled grass where three horses had waited out the hours of darkness.

Poker whistled shrilly and the other

riders came to his call. Warmed from riding and with their quarry's tracks still fresh, the posse took up the chase with relish. Red Corder slipped back to ride with the four hired guns.

'A hundred dollars extra to the man who brings down Jake Jefferson,' he told them. 'I don't want him brought back for no trial.'

Around noon a pale sun appeared, but the clouds still hung over the high country. Ahead of the riders the foothills rose, and for a brief moment something darker could be seen moving on the horizon; three tiny shapes were silhouetted against the washed-out sky. One of them turned sideways and became a man on a horse, then the three rode over the ridge and were gone.

'They're on Coyote Pass,' Red said exultantly. 'Ain't more'n five miles ahead!'

18

The night's rain came raging down the creek, white foam frothing over black rocks with a roar as loud as the storm that spawned it. A shallow beach of dark sand on the edge of the torrent, the one spot of calm amidst the chaos, showed clear tracks where three horses had gone into the river. Ketteridge squinted at the further shore. Three sets of prints showed where the riders had emerged safely on the other side. He cursed. Mitchell was getting all the luck.

'How'd they get through?' Rufe asked, shouting to make himself heard.

'It musta risen a foot since they was here,' Red told him.

'Reckon we can make it?' Ketteridge pushed his reluctant horse into the shallow water to stare at the turmoil beyond.

'Nope.' Red hauled his mount away. 'You wanna go that way you're on your own, Sheriff. I ain't tryin'. There's a place about two miles downstream, river's wider there. Still be fast but I never knowed it so's you couldn't cross.'

'We'll lose a lot of time.' Ketteridge was still hesitating.

'Sheriff?' It was Winterson, raising his voice over the din. 'The river marks the county line, you won't have authority once you cross.'

'Mitchell's a convicted murderer.' Ketteridge hauled on his rein and turned to face the judge. 'Are you saying you want me to let him go?'

'I'm saying once you cross the boundary you have to find a local marshal and get him to swear out a warrant. I admire your zeal, Sheriff, but this posse can only act within Douglas County.'

'We're wastin' time,' Rufe said. 'Jaw all you want, but I'm goin' after Mitchell an' Jefferson.'

'Boy's right.' Red nodded. 'Nobody ain't gonna argue with us for crossin' a line on some damn map when we're fetchin' ourselves a couple of murderers.'

The townsmen gathered around Winterson.

'If what you say's true, Judge, then we ain't going no further,' Gus Hallerfield said. 'Figure it's time to turn round.'

'I'm with you,' Big Pete agreed.

'You heard what Rufe said. It ain't just Mitchell,' Red Corder's voice rose. 'That whelp from the Lazy T killed Rollo.'

'Rollo shot the girl,' Hallerfield said. 'I saw it. An' he was sighting another shot. No matter what she done I don't like to see a man put a bullet in a female, it ain't right. Can't blame Jake for stoppin' him.'

'You're just afraid of Quentin Jefferson!' Red roared. 'You're a load of chicken-livered — '

'That's enough Red.' Ketteridge

looked round at the men ranged against him, his gaze eventually resting on the judge. 'I'm not quitting. The way I see it Jake Jefferson has to answer for shooting Rollo; it's up to us to bring him in for trial. Mitchell's a convicted murderer. If you're worried about keeping on the right side of the law we'll go find ourselves a marshal like you say, though it's likely to lose us a day getting a warrant sworn. Are you coming with me?'

Winterson shook his head.

'No. If you take my advice you'll turn around too.'

'What about the rest of you? Mitchell cheated the gallows. Seems to me Rollo Corder got himself killed trying to stop him getting away. Reckon it's up to us to put that straight.'

Only the Corders and their four hired men rode forward to join him.

'Seven against three,' Ketteridge said. 'No problem.' His eyes travelled briefly to Nat Grimes. The old man looked down, not meeting his eyes. Ketteridge nodded curtly and laid spurs to his horse. 'We'll be back in a few days.'

Winterson and the others turned back. After hesitating a moment Nat went after them, crowding on Hallerfield's heels.

'I figured you was here to see Bill Mitchell didn't end up with a bullet in his back, Gus,' he said. 'An' you, Hickory, you gonna leave him and Quentin's boy to get butchered by Corder's gunslingers?'

'They got a good start,' Hallerfield said. 'Bill can take care of hisself.'

'When he's already got a bullet in him?' Nat snarled. He spurred his horse to get in front of them, blocking their way. 'Well?'

'Don't reckon we could do much against them hired killers anyway.' Hallerfield shrugged. 'It's fine for you Nat, but we got businesses to run.'

'Gus is right,' Big Pete nodded. 'If I don't work my son and his family don't eat.'

'They'll string him up from a tree,'

Nat said. 'Bill deserves better'n that.'

'He was convicted and sentenced to hang,' Winterson said, setting his horse into motion. 'Ketteridge will keep the Corders reined in. He's doing his job.'

'The judge is right, there's nothing any of us can do,' Hickory Salmon said. 'Come on, Nat, let's go home.'

Nat Grimes pulled his horse aside and watched them ride away. Then, with a curse, he swung his horse's head round and galloped after Ketteridge. What was left of the posse was strung out along the riverbank, the water thundering at their side. Red Corder and the sheriff rode at the back and Nat came up behind them, unnoticed and unheard over the din of the tumbling water.

'It ain't no accident Mitchell headin' this way,' Red said, raising his voice so Ketteridge could hear him. 'Only one place he could be goin'.'

'Figured it right from the start,' Ketteridge called back. 'Mitchell knows what happened that night, or he's guessed; either way he'll be looking for proof. Could even be that interfering dude heard something from Ethan before I put the little runt out of his misery.'

The fingers of Nat's right hand slid from the rein to grip the butt of his rifle, anger building within him. He hadn't believed Palmer when he hinted that Ketteridge might have been the one who shot Ethan Jones, but it looked like he'd been right. And if the sheriff had killed Ethan to silence him, then what else was he hiding?

Red shook his head.

'Sure is strange Palmer turnin' out to be Billy Mitchell. Was barely a day when he an' my boys weren't fightin'; never thought he'd turn up an' rescue his old man, though; he hated him worse'n poison. Makes no sense. You reckon he got stopped at Pacetown?'

'It don't matter,' Ketteridge said. 'With Ethan dead he's got no evidence, not once we deal with Mitchell. Unless you or Rufe shoot your mouths off.' He paused. 'And you won't do that.'

'We ain't stupid. With your help the Jeffersons are finally gonna get what's comin' to 'em. They've kept holda that prairie way too long.' The river was growing quieter now, the valley widening out. Not far ahead rock gave way to grass. 'Ford's just past the next bend.' Red half-turned in the saddle and jerked back on the rein as he saw the rider behind them.

Too late Nat realized how stupid he'd been to go on following them. He hauled his horse around but Red was already on his tail, his hand on the Henry rifle in his saddle holster.

'We got trouble, Sheriff!'

Nat clapped his heels to his horse's sides and the grey leapt to a gallop, retracing its steps up the rocky slope they'd been descending, careless of the rough going. Leaning low over the horn Nat didn't look back, by the sound of it the whole shebang were after him; there was a cold prickle of fear down his spine as he waited for the crash of gunfire. Would he hear the shot before the bullet smashed into him?

He was almost back to the place where the fugitives had crossed the river and for a crazy moment he wondered if he should try to ford the raging water, but the men were gaining ground; if his horse hesitated they'd have him cold. He raked his spurs at the horse's flanks and angled left to get back on to the track they'd followed from Serenity. His only hope lay in catching up with Winterson.

As the thunder of the torrent faded behind him he heard the first shot, followed by Ketteridge's voice.

'Don't shoot,' he shouted. 'Run him down!'

Nat's grey faltered. He'd taken a risk in cutting off the corner and he was about to pay the price. A miniature ravine opened up across its path; the horse did its best to leap over the gap, but it misjudged the distance and landed short, falling in a spectacular tangle of flying hoofs. Nat was catapulted out of the saddle. His back slammed into the ground, driving the breath from his body. He was aware of the grey clambering up and running off without him.

The clatter of iron-shod feet came pounding up through the earth where he lay staring at the sky, clear blue and cloudless now. He had to move. Gulping at the air like a drowning man, somehow Nat managed to flip on to his stomach, his right hand groping for the Smith & Wesson he was wearing.

One of Corder's hired guns was closing, a savage grin lifting the corners of his mouth.

'You got him, Hollings,' Red Corder yelled. Hollings needed no encouragement. He spurred his horse, driving it to a flat gallop, grinning savagely at the old man who lay waiting helplessly for him, not seeing the gully that had brought down Nat's grey. The horse suddenly threw its weight back on its haunches and skidded to a halt on the edge of the drop, throwing up loose rock and sand and nearly dislodging its rider.

Nat was ready, holding a painful breath to keep the Smith & Wesson steady. Hollings' grin froze as he flailed wildly at the air to keep his balance. Nat fired and the grin disappeared, along with half the man's face, flesh and bone erupting into a bloody mess as the bullet took him beneath one eye. With its rider slumping back in the saddle the horse plunged sideways and the body slid bonelessly to one side. His right foot was still in the stirrup-iron and he hung there like a child's rag-doll.

Squealing in terror at the reek of blood the beast reared. Unable to dislodge its unfamiliar burden it bolted, with Hollings's battered head thudding against the ground at each step. The rest of the horses caught its mindless panic and they scattered, their riders cursing as they fought to regain control.

It was a gift Nat hadn't dared hope

for. He was breathing easier now and there was time to sight the shot, though with the horses milling there were no easy targets. He drew a bead on Poker's chest. As he fired Ritchie, another of the Corder hired guns, drove his horse at the gully, pushing Poker aside. Nat didn't see what happened to his shot because by then Ritchie had leapt from his saddle and was right beside him. Nat fired again. Roaring with anger Ritchie kicked the gun from Nat's hand then stamped on his wrist.

Pain exploded up Nat's arm as his bones shattered, but he wasn't finished. Gritting his teeth he flung his left hand across to pick up the Smith & Wesson, screaming with the pain of his mangled wrist but rolling away with the gun butt settling into his palm. He fired wildly until the hammer clicked on an empty chamber. Firing left-handed from the ground he doubted if a single bullet had hit home but he'd made a lot of noise, there was just a chance Winterson and the others would hear the gunfire.

Ritchie's boot connected with the side of Nat's head. The world tilted and spun, a vast array of coloured lights shot across Nat's sight, searing his whole head with an incredible agony. He barely felt the second blow: he was already slipping away, floating in a world of white fog and swirling water. Strange, he thought vaguely, the morning mist coming back that way when a moment ago he'd seen a clear sky. Ritchie drew back his foot for the last time.

'Damn the old fool!' Red's furious words were the last thing Nat heard. He slipped down into the welcoming darkness with a smile on his lips.

19

Ritchie and Ketteridge threw Nat's body into the creek. For a moment the dead weight caught on a rock, then it rolled sluggishly, one arm lifting in a bizarre wave before the body was taken by the current, rushing downstream on a tide of turbulent white foam.

'Shoulda saved a piece of him for me,' Poker complained, tightening his neckerchief over the slash Nat's bullet had ploughed across his thigh. 'This hurts like hell.'

'Count yourself lucky it's a flesh wound,' Ketteridge said curtly, 'we're a long way from a doctor.'

Red Corder appeared and pulled up beside Poker.

'You fit to ride?'

'I can ride. But we're a horse short.' Poker gestured at where Ritchie's mount lay in a pool of blood, a last trickle still oozing slowly from the wound beneath its jaw.

'What happened out there?' Ketteridge asked.

'Horse went loco. Fell in a hole an' broke its fool neck,' Red said. 'I left Whitey pilin' rocks over what's left of Hollings.'

'Rufe went after the grey the old man was riding.' Ketteridge said. 'But I want to get moving. Nat Grimes cost us a lot of time, don't figure to waste no more.'

Red nodded.

'Ritchie, you wait here for Rufe an' Whitey. If they don't catch the grey you'll have to ride double. We gotta get after Mitchell; we don't want him making it to China Wells.'

'What's at China Wells?' Poker asked, hobbling to his roan.

'State penitentiary,' Ketteridge said shortly.

'That's crazy.' Poker heaved himself into the saddle. 'Mitchell just escaped from the rope an' he's headin' for a prison?'

'He's lookin' for Spurs Osgood,' Red said, turning his horse to follow the track downstream again. 'An' that's one man we don't want him to find.'

'Been thinking about that.' Ketteridge pushed his horse alongside. 'No point following their trail any longer. If we aim clear to the north soon as we cross the river we'll hit the plain sooner, maybe head them off.'

Once they were through the ford they picked up a faint depression sloping down out of the foothills; though the track didn't look to have been used in a long time the going was easier and the weary horses increased their pace. Soon the plain was stretched out before them, the sparse vegetation parched to a dull gold, untouched by the rain. Far off a cluster of buildings lay like a dark stain on the featureless landscape.

'That's where they're headed,' Ketteridge said. 'China Wells penitentiary.' He pulled up as hoofbeats sounded behind them. Rufe appeared, his palomino followed by Ritchie mounted on Nat Grimes's grey; both horses were flecked with white foam on neck and flanks.

'Where's Whitey?' Red asked.

'He's comin',' Rufe said. 'Horse threw a shoe.'

'They can't be far ahead now.' Ketteridge stared out over the plain.

'There!' Rufe pointed exultantly. 'We got 'em.' A tiny dark dot was moving down towards the plain.

'Just one.' Ketteridge reached into his saddlebag. He brought a telescope and lifted it. 'Looks like Mitchell.' The horse was sending up a spray of dust as it slid down the last slope, and its head dipped suddenly. As the horse almost fell the rider flung up an arm to keep his balance and the wide-brimmed hat flew off his head. Ketteridge stared through the telescope and swore.

'What?' Red was impatient, kneeing his mount out on to the baked dirt. 'We're wastin' time.'

'That's what we've been doing these last two days,' Ketteridge said, handing over the glass. 'Take a look. Unless Mitchell's hair turned back to brown I'd say we're following the wrong man.'

'But it sure looks like him. Young Jefferson's built like a girl . . . It's Palmer!' Red spat the word and thrust the telescope back at Ketteridge. 'Come on, we'll cut him off.'

The sheriff shook his head.

'It's Mitchell we want, not the dude.' He turned his horse round.

'You figure he's hidin' out back there?' Red nodded at the foothills. 'We was followin' three riders.'

'I doubt it. I reckon he never went more'n a few miles from Serenity. But we'd best check. I ain't planning to be made a fool of twice.'

'What about him?' Rufe objected, staring out where the solitary rider was racing across the flats. 'I got some old scores to settle with Billy Mitchell. An' you don't want him talkin' to Osgood.'

'What he hears won't do him no good once Mitchell's dead.' Red was blunt. 'Besides, I'm more interested in findin' the Jefferson kid.'

'We'll split up,' Ketteridge said. 'Me Red and Poker'll back-track to where Palmer hit the plain, the rest of you cut across and try an' find their trail from the river.'

'One thing,' Ritchie said, pulling his horse around to follow Rufe. 'Just so I got this clear. You plannin' to take anyone back to that fancy hangin' tree you built?'

'You heard what the judge said,' Ketteridge replied. 'We ain't a posse no more.' With that he clapped spurs to his tired horse.

★ ★ ★

Jake Jefferson stood in the mouth of the cave and watched the men and horses far below.

'They've seen Billy. A lot of them must've turned back at the river, there's only six left.' He frowned. 'They just split up but it doesn't look like any of them are following him.'

241

Flame came to stand behind him, tying the fresh bandage she'd wrapped round her arm.

'Then we don't have to worry about him getting to China Wells.'

'No.' He stood up. 'All we have to worry about is all six of them coming to look for us. I'd better get those horses hidden. Are you all right? Falling like that . . .'

'The horse fell,' she pointed out sharply.

'Yeah, but it made that crease start bleeding again.'

'It's fine, it's healing clean. I could have gone on.'

'Not on that horse,' Jake said. 'He needs rest even more than you.' He looked around the cave. 'Reckon I could bring them up here, sun's moved. We're in shadow now and it'll be dark in a couple of hours.' He drew the Navy Colt from its holster and checked the chambers.

Flame picked up the Winchester she'd left by the entrance.

'Mind they don't see you. I'd be happy to put a bullet in Rufe, and maybe Red too if I was pushed to it, but I don't think I can cope with six.' She looked up from wiping a speck of dirt off the foresight. 'What're you smiling at?'

'You're not like any other girl I ever met,' Jake said.

'You mean I'm not much of a lady. But then I'm a Corder,' she added acidly.

He shook his head, refusing to rise to the challenge.

'I mean I couldn't see Daisy Salmon helping rescue a man from the rope.'

Flame tossed her head.

'How about Kate? A girl who'll take the name of Corder isn't short on courage. She lost a lot of friends the day she married Thaddeus.'

The smile slipped from Jake's face.

'You know I always admired Kate. But she wouldn't have me.'

She was silent a while, looking at him.

'He's a good man,' she said at last, 'not much like the rest of them.'

'We wouldn't have got this far without his help,' Jake admitted. 'I won't be long.' Before she could utter another word of caution he'd gone.

Flame lay back on her bedroll and stared at the rock above her head. Her eyes were heavy with weariness but she didn't want to sleep. The image of a man came into her mind, a stocky broad-shouldered man with a spoiled face; some women might find him ugly, but right from the start she'd barely noticed the scar. To her he was the boy whose eyes met hers in the sheriff's house all those years ago.

A few months after that meeting she'd been sent back to her father. He'd found a place to live in Montana; nobody was looking for him that far north. There'd been five more years of scraping a living, hiding from the law, running when they couldn't pay their debts. Through it all he'd been there in the back of her mind, the boy with the angry grey eyes.

Her lips curved into a smile as sleep crept up on her. The fingers that had been curled over the butt of her father's Winchester relaxed and she turned to settle on her side, facing away from the fading daylight.

'Got you, bitch!' Brought awake so brutally Flame tried to scream but there was a hand on her throat, so close to throttling her that her newly opened eyes saw through a fog of pain. Her hands flailed wildly, feeling for the Winchester. Something cold and hard was thrust against her cheek. 'Lookin' for this?'

She went limp, her eyes rolling up into her head. At once the pressure on her neck eased. Rufe had released her, muttering curses as he looked around the cave. Flame breathed shallowly, trying not to let him see how much each breath hurt. Intent on convincing him she'd passed out, she let her eyelids droop so that she could see out from beneath them. He was coming back.

Selecting a target she tensed her leg muscles. As she slammed upwards with both feet she felt the blow go home, but she'd missed Rufe's groin; he'd seen the kick coming and turned, taking it on his thigh. A flicker of fear raced through her; Rufe wasn't the forgiving kind. She gulped in a breath and steeled herself to fight.

Flame rolled, half-way to getting up, trying to snatch the Winchester out of her cousin's hand. She got her fingers to the barrel, her other hand out-stretched towards his face, long nails reaching for his eyes. Rufe swept the rifle out of her grasp, then brought it raking down her arm. She let out a muffled squeal between clenched teeth, dropping back on to the bedroll. In two days the wound had hardly troubled her, now it felt as if the whole of her right side was on fire.

Rufe tossed the gun away and dropped down on top of her.

'That's where I like a woman,' he said, his lips drawn back in a travesty of a smile. 'On her back an' ready an' waitin', but you go ahead an' fight all you want. Just makes it sweeter in the end.'

She tried to think past the agony running up to her shoulder; her arm and fingers had gone numb, they were useless. With the Winchester gone the only weapons left to her were those Rufe brought with him. He'd already taken off his gun belt; he must have been there quite a time, watching her sleep. That left his knife.

Flame's left hand crept round Rufe's back, but before she could locate the sheath her fingers were caught in a rough grip and squeezed hard. Tears of pain forced their way from between her closed eyelids, though she fought to stop them, furious that he might think he'd made her cry.

'They say you're too much for me to handle,' Rufe said, taking her chin in his hand. 'What you reckon, huh?' His breath was foul in her nose and throat as he clamped his mouth over hers.

Frantically she stamped down on her fear; her legs were beneath his, she kicked but couldn't get enough power behind the blow to hurt him.

She held her jaw clamped shut as he tried to open her mouth with his lips and tongue but then he grabbed her upper lip between his teeth and bit hard. The pain of it made her gasp and he grinned. She spat at him, blood and spittle taking him full in the face.

Rufe let go of her chin and brought his hand across to slap her face, putting all his strength into the blow. Flame's head jerked around with the force of it and her senses reeled. She lay still as he ripped the shirt down from her throat, groping over her stomach, wrenching at the men's pants she wore. He was breathing hard, sweat beading his face.

'Goddam bitch,' he grated, as the waistband refused to tear. 'Don't even dress like a woman!' He reached behind his back for the knife.

20

Palmer sent his mount slithering precariously down the last steep slope, its head in the air, scrabbling feet sending a great dust-cloud billowing skywards. It almost fell and he flung up a hand to keep his balance, giving the exhausted animal a chance to recover its footing. He didn't notice the borrowed hat fly from his head. Keeping ahead of the posse was all that mattered; he'd seen the three riders reach the plain. With its hoofs on the level baked earth the horse obediently flattened out in a gallop, racing for the distant buildings.

Out of the corner of his eye he thought he saw movement. He leant forward, willing the horse to go faster; its breath was roaring, head nodding wearily as it gave him the last of its strength. Risking a backward glance

Palmer sucked in a breath; there was nobody following him. He checked the horse and it eased back gratefully, its strides breaking up into an unco-ordinated jog. Palmer stared at the foothills. Nothing moved. Then he noticed that his head was bare, realized the men must have recognized him. He'd expected the posse to follow him to China Wells to try to stop him seeing Spurs Osgood.

The horse stood with its head down. It was covered in sweat and its legs trembled with fatigue. For a long moment Palmer hesitated, worrying about Flame, then he climbed achingly out of the saddle and started walking, dragging the reluctant beast behind him. The dusty brown shadows became solid walls as the prison reared up through the afternoon haze. It had the look of a fort, the wide gateway guarded by two towers. He'd been seen and the heavy gate swung open as he limped the last few yards.

Standing facing the armed guards

inside the gate Palmer felt in his vest pocket, drawing out a piece of card.

'I'm from the *Eastern Gazette*. I've got urgent business with the governor.' From another pocket he took out a few coins. 'Be grateful if somebody could tend this horse for me.'

The darkness came on with a rush, time passing in a blur. The governor's office was warmed by the flickering lamp on the desk. Palmer sat, fighting sleep, biting down hard on his lips and staring at the woven screen that had been dragged across in front of him, dividing the room. The pattern shimmered.

Palmer tried to focus on the paper before him. There were two sheets filled with his small handwriting, questions and answers that held the key to a man's life. From behind the screen the governor's voice echoed strangely and Palmer shook himself; he had what he'd come for; all he had to do was stay awake until it was time to leave, then the fresh prairie air would revive him.

' . . . if you're sure,' Spurs Osgood said, his voice coming from just beyond the screen. 'But there's more if you want to hear it.'

Palmer's drooping eyes were suddenly wide open. He picked up the pen that had fallen from his fingers and dipped it into the ink.

'Something else happened that night?' Governor Wendall asked. Palmer wrote down the question and waited.

'I'll tell if it's worth something. Seems you're interested in that deputy who was supposed to be guarding me. You know he went missing, but suppose I tell you what he said to the lame brain when he came back?' Osgood's tone became ingratiating. 'That's gotta be worth hearing. I'm not asking much. It's hard on that rock pile and I'm getting along in years, Governor.'

'I doubt if anything important would have been said in front of you.' Wendall was dismissive. 'And it was quite a few weeks ago. How can I be sure you remember?'

'My memory's real good. And they didn't know I was listening. When a man's served as much time as I have, he gets to know a trick or two.' A low rhythmic sound issued from his throat, not exactly a snore, but the loud steady breathing of a man deeply asleep. Osgood laughed briefly. 'I can do that for an hour at a time, get to hear some mighty interesting things that way.'

'Humph,' the governor grunted. 'All right, tell me.'

'How 'bout that rock pile?'

'I'll think about it.'

'You're a fair man, Governor, guess I can trust you. This is how it was. The runt was nervous, kept pacing up and down and chewing on his fingers. By the time the deputy came back he was ready to wet his pants. He started shouting like he was mad about something, but he kept falling over his words so nothing he said made much sense. The deputy slapped a hand over his mouth to shut him up. 'It went fine, he's all sewn up,' he said. 'You get your two hundred tomorrow. Just remember we were here together all night'.'

'It that it?' the governor asked.

'That's it. The lame brain still wasn't happy, but he shut up. I didn't know what it was all about, still don't. No chance you want to tell me I suppose?'

'None. All right, guard, take him back to his cell. And reassign him, find him a job in the kitchen. Then get back here.'

There was the sound of a chair being pushed back and the governor came around the screen.

'You've got your answers, Mr Palmer,' he said. 'If I hadn't heard it myself I wouldn't have believed it, the case against Mitchell looked pretty solid according to all the reports. Obviously the deputy robbed the bank and the other man provided him with an alibi. Since Osgood was collected by a couple of deputies from Denver the next morning there was nobody to discredit their story.' He took the papers Palmer had written. 'I'll read through these, then the guard and I will sign them.'

'Thank you,' Palmer forced himself to his feet. 'Is there any chance of finding fresh horses here?'

'Apart from the half-dozen mounts we keep for our own use there's nothing closer than twenty miles.' He led the way to the door. 'It's too dark to travel tonight, and by the look of you you're in as much need of rest as your horse. Norris will show you where you can sleep.'

'I can't stay,' Palmer protested. 'I've left two friends hiding in the foothills and Ketteridge is out there.'

'But neither you nor he will be able to find them until first light, there's no moon. I'll make sure you're woken before dawn.' The governor smiled as Palmer swayed on his feet. 'How far do you think you'd get before you fell asleep?'

★ ★ ★

At his second attempt Rufe sliced through the waistband of Flame's pants. His mouth was hanging open and his hands were unsteady; the blade nicked her flesh. Thick and noisy, his breathing echoed round the walls. Flame lay quiescent beneath him, her eyes staring past the pale oval of his face and the fever-bright eyes at the shadowed roof of the cave beyond. The daylight had almost gone. She told herself she was saving her strength; she could still fight, but she'd bide her time until she had at least a chance of success.

With slow deliberation Rufe tore her pants away, ripping the material down the length. A small animal sound came from him and he licked his lips.

'Rufe?' The shout came from outside the cave and he paused, one warm sweaty hand gripping the top of her drawers, the other holding the knife, ready to cut the flimsy material away. His fingers were hot against her cold flesh. As if in warning he moved the blade up so that it pressed lightly against her breast. He stared at the tiny bead of blood that appeared at its tip and his tongue flicked over his lips again.

'Rufe?' She recognized the voice. It was the man they called Whitey.

Rufe swallowed hard, his pale-blue eyes unfocused.

'What?'

'You in there? Your pa's signallin', there's a man ridin' up the hill, could be Jefferson. We got him cold!'

'Be right there,' Rufe called. 'You get goin'.' He hauled in a deep breath then sliced strips off her ruined shirt to tie her hands behind her back. When it was done her naked breasts were thrust forward and he stared at them hungrily, unable to resist taking them in his dirty hands, pressing them together so hard that it hurt, then he shook himself, releasing her and rocking back on his heels.

'One thing about livin' with Pa, you sure learn patience. Be all the sweeter when I get back, won't it, honey.'

Flame gritted her teeth, her hatred strong enough to choke on.

He tied her ankles together.

'Just in case you ain't willin' to wait for me, darlin',' he said, pulling at the knots then stroking a rough hand up her calf and round to the inside of her thigh. He pushed up the white lace trim on her drawers, the only garment he'd left her. 'I'll be back soon as I dealt with Jefferson. That's who it is, right?'

She stared defiantly up at him, saying nothing. Rufe grinned.

'Hell, if it was anyone but Jake out there I swear I couldn't bring myself to go. Just beg me to stay an' I'll leave him to Pa and the others. Maybe if they catch him alive I'll bring him along. He can watch you an' me have our fun, a kinda goin'-away present before I kill him.'

'You think you're such a big man, Rufe.' She spat bloody spittle at his face. 'But you're nothing. You never were and you never will be.'

The grin melted off his face and he hit her a stinging blow across the mouth. Her brutalized lip screamed a protest but she bit back on the sound, clamping her teeth together.

Rufe took hold of a handful of her hair and pulled.

'That's the last time you talk to me that way. You're gonna treat me right, girl, or when I'm done I'll hand you over to the boys, let 'em all have a taste of you.' He stood up, tossing the bedroll and the saddlebags away from her before he strode out of the cave.

Once he'd gone Flame twisted her head, trying to locate her saddlebags in the increasing gloom. They'd landed against the far wall of the cave. She jerked her abused body across the rocky floor like a wounded snake, shuddering as the rough surface grated against her bare flesh. Her hands and feet were so cold she could hardly feel them; she only knew she'd reached the wall when her head struck the rock. She squirmed around until she felt the worn leather beneath her hands.

Uttering a prayer of thanks that she'd left the bags open, Flame explored the contents with numb fingers until they encountered the bone handle of her knife.

The blade was razor-sharp. It wasn't easy to cut through bonds that she couldn't see, with her fingers almost frozen, but somehow she must be gone when Rufe returned. At last the material parted and she was free, though her hands were bleeding in a dozen places. She sat up to release her ankles and tossed the scraps of cloth aside, revolted by the thought of Rufe's hands on them; she wanted to run to the river and scrub at her flesh to erase the memory of his touch. Delving again into the saddlebag she brought out a shirt and pants, her whole body shaking as if she'd been immersed in ice.

Once she was dressed Flame tucked the knife into her belt and gathered up her canteen and bedroll. The Winchester lay where Rufe had tossed it. She explored it with shaking hands, then moved to the mouth of the cave where the last faint glimmer of daylight lingered. The Winchester's barrel was bent. The tears she'd left unshed before gathered in her eyes. It had been her father's gun, about the only thing he'd left her.

As Flame ducked out of the cave she heard a single rifle shot from the hillside somewhere below, followed by a shout of triumph. Rufe must have found Jake. Flame swept her tongue across her bloody lip and shuddered. She was unarmed and alone. There was only one thing left to do. She ran.

21

'He's gotta be here.' Rufe Corder rode the palomino through the tangle of rocks, his rifle angled down at the deep shadows around the horse's feet.

'Could be he throwed hisself clear an' ran,' Ritchie suggested, circling wider away from the place where they'd seen the rider fall and peering at the ground. 'Was it Jefferson?'

'Ain't no way I'd mistake that skinny little runt,' Rufe said. 'Hey, Pa!' Three riders were coming slowly up the hill, picking their way in the growing darkness. 'I plugged Jefferson, but he musta fell down a hole someplace.'

'You sure you hit him?' Ketteridge pulled up, staring into the gloom. 'Light's bad.'

Whitey rode up to them then, leading two horses behind his own.

'There's a splash of fresh blood on

the saddle,' he said. 'Rufe hit him right enough.'

'What about the other one?' Ketteridge asked.

'She's safe,' Rufe said, grinning. 'Waitin' for me to go join her. Figure we'll celebrate our weddin' night a few days early.'

'She?' Red Corder stared at his son.

'Yeah. It's Flame.'

Red shook his head.

'Never thought that girl would let her own folks down that way.'

'Maybe she fell for Jake. Sure would like to finish him for certain. He's gotta be here someplace.'

'He'll keep till mornin'; he ain't goin' nowhere without a horse,' Red said. 'Figure we'll wait out the night here. Let's get a fire lit before it gets too damn dark to see.'

'I'm goin' back to my girl,' Rufe said. 'Had to put a rope on her, she's wild as a mustang with burrs in her tail, but I swear she'll be tame as a yeller dog by mornin'.'

'Put the horses up against the hill. We'll set a guard,' Ketteridge said. He looked up at Rufe, still mounted on the palomino. 'You'd best leave that cayuse here, seeing as how you'll be busy. Just in case Jefferson isn't hit that bad.'

Rufe shrugged and lit down.

'Sure. Maybe I'll wait an' take me a bit of fire.' He grinned. 'Wouldn't like Flame to miss seein' what's comin' to her.'

By the time he'd climbed up towards the cave with a glowing brand of wood held at arm's length before him, the night was black without even a star to lighten the sky. At the cave's mouth he thrust the torch into a clump of tinder-dry thorn. The bush crackled and flared, sending sparks high into the air. Rufe laughed.

'Got it all lit up for you darlin',' he called. 'Just like the fourth of July.'

He walked inside, still holding the torch, the light sending his shadow racing round the walls of the empty cave and showing the scraps of cloth lying on the rocky floor. Rufe cursed long and loud, then ran back outside.

★ ★ ★

By dawn Palmer was half-way back across the plain. He'd struck a deal with a guard; the little bay he rode was only half-broke but it was all he could get; just so long as he didn't fall off. He scanned the foothills before him for signs of life. The posse was out there somewhere. They could be half-way to the county line, speeding back towards Serenity. Or they could be waiting for him.

Lifting a hand he touched the bulge in his vest where he carried the bundle of papers the governor had signed; he had to get it back to the judge before Ketteridge caught up with Bill Mitchell, but he didn't like the idea of abandoning Flame and Jake. He began to climb and the horse slowed. Above him nothing moved but a wisp of smoke spiralling lazily into the still morning air. As he turned to head towards it the horse's shoulders and haunches strained to pull up a steep shelf of rock.

'Lookin' for somebody, Billy?' Rufe stood on the slope above, a rifle at his shoulder, his eye to the sights.

'You'll do, Rufe.' Palmer stepped down, looping the reins over the saddle horn. 'I know what happened the night Stein was killed, but I'd just like to get the last couple of details clear in my mind. What did you see when you looked in through that window?'

Rufe laughed.

'Reckon I can tell you, ain't as if you're gonna be gabbin' to nobody. I saw Ketteridge holdin' a gun on Stein while the old man opened the safe. It was like drawin' a royal flush. Hell, you shoulda seen Rollo when I told him 'bout Ketteridge settin' the sheriff up. He laughed so hard I figured he'd bust somethin'. We was finally gonna give the Jeffersons what they've bin dishin' out to us. The Lazy T's finished.

Quentin Jefferson's nothin' without Bill Mitchell.'

He climbed down the hill towards Palmer, working the bolt on the rifle.

'Anythin' else you wanna know? Me an' Flame got real well acquainted last night, maybe you'd like to send her your goodbyes? Shame you won't be around to see us get wed. I'm plannin' a real big affair.'

Palmer's hands clenched into fists but his scarred face gave nothing away.

'Same old Rufe,' he said evenly. 'All mouth.' He opened his coat to show he carried no weapon. 'You don't even have the guts to face an unarmed man without a gun in your hands.'

'No?' Rufe laid the rifle down, then unbuckled his gun belt. 'Just you watch me, Billy boy. I came close to killin' you before, ain't no girl to bring you help this time.'

As the holster touched the ground Palmer leapt, throwing himself at Rufe and sending him sprawling in the dust, following him down, fists flying fast to deny him the advantage of his longer reach. He landed a solid blow on the redhead's jaw and jabbed another at his ribs. A bunch of sinewy fingers came reaching for his face, clawing at his eyes. Palmer twisted his head and sank his teeth into the filthy thumb as it gouged his scarred cheek. With a yell Rufe pulled away, his right hand whipping round behind his back.

Palmer drove in hard, making every blow count. Pain sliced suddenly into his hand and he jerked it away; there was a bloody line scored across his knuckles. Rufe had aimed to thrust the knife in below his ribs but chance had put Palmer's fist there instead. Rolling clear Palmer pushed to his feet, retreating fast, but Rufe followed with a grin on his face, the blade swishing as he sliced at the air.

'All mouth, you reckon? I got teeth, dude.'

Flinging up his elbow to block a blow Palmer lunged to meet him half-way, grabbing an ear along with a hank of red hair and twisting hard, dragging Rufe off balance, sending his knife hand flying wide. Stamping his boot down with all his strength on Rufe's leg, Palmer felt the bone give and heard the dull crack as it snapped.

Rufe yelled as much in fury as in pain. He pulled free, leaving some hair and a scrap of bloody flesh in Palmer's hand. Throwing his weight on to his good leg to stay upright he thrust up hard with the knife.

There was no time to dodge. Palmer had expected Rufe to fall, he'd been ready to slam down across the man's body. Instead he was caught wrong-footed and Rufe's knife hand was already inside his guard, the glittering steel coming fast. In desperation Palmer wrapped his fingers around the blade as it slid between his ribs, the sharp edge searing into his flesh. The hilt ground into the side of his hand as Rufe sought for his heart.

When they fell Palmer was underneath but he still held the knife, fighting the pain as the razor-sharp edges sliced into his fingers, keeping the sliver of steel from penetrating deeper into his chest. His other hand reached blindly for his enemy's face, groping for his eyes, his throat, seeking for a hold to push Rufe away.

''Bye Billy,' Rufe breathed, his lips twisting in a savage grin. Ignoring the fingers clamped round his neck he put both hands on the hilt of the knife and bore down with all his weight. Palmer gritted his teeth and thrashed with his feet. He was rewarded by a yelp of rage and pain, but the pressure on the knife didn't ease and the blade crept deeper between his ribs.

Rufe's howl became a savage exultation. It could be the last sound Palmer heard. In sheer desperation he struck at Rufe's face with all the strength left to him, muscles bunching in his shoulder to slice the side of his hand above that crowing mouth. The sound was abruptly shut off. Rufe sagged. Slowly a hot dribble of blood slid from between his lips to land on Palmer's cheek.

Palmer heaved, pushing Rufe off him, scarcely believing it when the body fell limp and heavy to the ground. He took his mangled hand from the knife. The wound in his chest began throbbing in time with his pounding heart; there was a lot of blood, but most of it came from his fingers. He put his right hand to the weapon's hilt and pulled, ignoring the crescendo of pain as the flesh clung to the steel, reluctant to let it go. A trickle of blood followed the blade as it tore free but there was no cascade of red; he wasn't dying.

Pressing his lacerated left hand over the wound Palmer crawled to Rufe. Dust was settling on the sightless eyes and the smiling mouth was strangely misshapen; only a smear of blood showed how he died.

'Billy,' Flame stood a few feet from him, gasping for breath as if she'd run a long way. Rufe's Smith & Wesson hung from her fingers. She dropped it as Palmer rose slowly to go to her.

Dirt and blood smirched her cheeks. Her top lip was discoloured and puffy with dark bloody scabs, while her hair was coated in dust, dull as a mustang's tail. He could see bruises on her neck too, running down beneath her shirt.

'Rufe?' he asked, fury rising to choke him.

She nodded. 'But he didn't . . . he didn't . . . ' she said, and suddenly she was in his arms and sobbing like a child. 'He broke Pa's gun.' He stroked her hair with a blood-stained hand, then lifted her chin so he could see her face. Her eyes were green pools, deep enough to drown in. Abruptly she pulled free, dashing the tears from her face with a grimy hand, touching the bloody stain on his vest.

'You're hurt.'

'Yeah,' he drawled, 'but unlike Rufe I'm alive.' Then they were in each other's arms again, laughing as if he'd said something funny. His hands were shaking; the warm scent of her body making his senses reel. He had to clench his smarting hand into a fist to keep from finishing what Rufe had started. This time he was the one who pulled away.

Flame's face flushed.

'I'd better take care of those cuts.'

'What happened to Jake?' Palmer asked, as she bound up his wounds.

'I don't know. He went to hide the horses, then Rufe found me.' She coloured again and dropped her eyes from his gaze. 'I fell asleep. I was almost as mad at myself as I was at Rufe. Anyway, one of Red's men called him away, and a bit later I heard a shot. They found our horses. If Jake got away he's on foot.'

'You're sure Red and the others have gone?'

'Yes. It was only Rufe who stayed to wait for you. And look for me,' she added. 'I watched the rest of them leave, they'll be half-way to the county line by now. What about Jake?'

'We find him.'

It was Flame who noticed the tiny

drops in the dust, dried black by the sun. She called Palmer and they followed the traces until the trail came to an end amid a tangle of narrow canyons.

'Jake!' Palmer shouted.

'Here.' The call came hoarsely from a gap in the rocks. They pulled Jake out of the crack, marvelling that he'd somehow fitted himself into such a narrow space. He was almost too weak to help himself, one leg trailing, his pants soaked in blood.

'I squeezed in there when I heard Rufe coming,' Jake said, as Flame tended his thigh; the bullet had gone straight through, breaking the bone on its way. The gaping exit wound was still bleeding. 'Guess I passed out for a while.' He shuddered. 'Sure was glad to hear you Billy, thought maybe I'd buried myself for good.' As soon as Flame had bound the wound, using her father's broken rifle as a splint, he tried to stand, but she pushed him back down. 'We have to get moving,' he protested, 'I heard them talking. They Figure Bill Mitchell's at the Lazy T. Pa's gonna need me.'

'You're going nowhere until this stops bleeding,' she said.

'I'll go,' Palmer said, looking at Flame. 'Do you think you can get him to China Wells?'

'No.' Jake grabbed Palmer's arm. 'I'm coming with you.'

'You'd never get to Serenity alive,' Flame said. 'You'll be no good to your pa in a wooden box. We'll ride as soon as we can. Billy's right, he'd better go on alone. Once the judge knows the truth the whole town's likely to turn out and settle with Ketteridge.'

22

Palmer hit the ground hard. The impact woke him and he grunted, squinting up at the horse; after nearly two days riding it had learned some manners and it stood patiently as he climbed back into the saddle. Even the steady throb from the wound between his ribs was no longer enough to hold his need for sleep at bay. He removed the stopper from his canteen and poured the contents over his head.

Spluttering but awake, he slapped back stiffly with his heels. The bay heaved itself into a reluctant gallop, and they came fast out of the belt of cottonwoods. A thick column of smoke rose into the air less than a quarter of a mile distant; somewhere beneath it lay the Lazy T. A man sat a horse on the track ahead, barring the way.

'Bad place to be, Billy.'

Palmer looked into the bony face, so like Rufe's and yet unlike.

'I could say the same to you, Thaddeus.'

'My pa's down there. Him and Rufe's family.'

'Not any more,' Palmer said. 'Rufe's dead.'

The pale blue eyes chilled to ice.

'You killed him.'

'He gave me no choice. If you'd seen what he did to Flame maybe you'd have done the same.'

'She hurt bad?'

'Nothing that won't heal. But Jake might not make it.'

The rattle of gunfire reached them, born on a sudden gust of wind.

'Man don't choose his family,' Thaddeus Corder said bleakly.

'You chose Kate,' Palmer reminded him. 'And she's going to need you once that baby's born. It's time to end this, Thad.' He took the bundle of papers from his pocket. 'I'd be grateful if you'd take these to Judge Winterson, ask him

277

to bring some help out here, and fast.'

With a nod Thaddeus Corder pulled his horse aside and took the papers.

'Don't figure Pa's gonna stop short of gettin' hisself killed, Billy, but . . . ' The words trailed off.

'I'll do what I can,' Palmer said. Corder nodded, turned his back on the Lazy T and kicked his horse to a gallop.

The bunkhouse was blazing, flames flickering along the roof and leaping from broken windows. Palmer coughed as the acrid taste of smoke hit the back of his tongue. A renewed burst of gunfire told him there was still some resistance, but time was running out for Quentin Jefferson. The fire had spread to the side of the ranch house.

Red Corder had men inside the barn, front and back, while others had taken cover behind the water-trough and the wagon standing by the corral. There was somebody climbing awkwardly out through the side window of the house, a stocky figure, broad in the shoulders and with a shock of grey hair.

Palmer kicked his weary horse and slashed the reins across its neck to send it careering between the barn and the blazing bunkhouse. He yelled, a wordless scream of defiance to draw the attackers' attention away from the figure crouching dangerously close to the flaming wall with a long-barrelled six-gun in his hand.

A gust of wind sent smoke billowing into Palmer's path. The bay leapt through it, hoofs pounding, nostrils flared in terror as sparks lodged in its mane. Palmer knocked them away and drove the beast on, the crackle of rifle fire exploding from his left. Figures moved eerily in the haze, one looming up almost under the bay's feet. Palmer swept down with his fist and the man fell, but the bay baulked and swerved, dropping its shoulder. The world spun as Palmer somersaulted.

As he rolled to his feet something whistled past his cheek, too close for comfort. He ran, hearing more bullets zipping by; he didn't need to feel the invisible hand pluck at his sleeve to tell him they were close. Blinded by smoke he stopped dead as he came up against something solid that grunted as he hit. They fell together against the wall of the barn and he found himself staring down the barrel of a Colt Peacemaker. Behind the gun loomed a familiar face.

'Billy! That was you.' Bill Mitchell still looked pale and drawn, and his left hand was clamped tight over the stain on his vest. 'Damn fool thing to do, though you probably saved my hide. Where's your gun?'

'I don't carry one.' Palmer squirmed. Something hard was digging into his back. He got a hand to it, and pulled out a broken axe-handle. 'Never found the need,' he added cheerfully, fitting his fist round the well worn shaft.

'You on your own? Didn't you fetch us some help from town?'

'If I had nobody would be here for another couple of hours,' Palmer pointed out as he sat up. The ranch house was well alight now, and the firing on both sides was continuous, though it was doubtful anyone could see what they were shooting at.

'Got a point,' Mitchell conceded.

'I saw Spurs Osgood. The proof's on its way to Serenity. It's enough to put a noose round Slim Ketteridge's neck.'

Mitchell looked at him, his forehead creasing as he studied the proud flesh pulled tight over the old wound on the younger man's face.

'Thanks, son. It's a damn sight more'n I deserve. It's late to be saying sorry, but . . .'

Palmer shook his head.

'Mom had it right, it wasn't your fault. I had a lot of growing up to do. Or maybe we were just too much alike.'

A bullet ricocheted off the wall over their heads. Bill Mitchell smiled.

'Guess this ain't the time an' place for a conversation. Quentin's arranging a diversion. You'd best stay here while I go and clear the vermin out of the barn.' Without another word he'd gone, crouching low to make the most of the drifting smoke. Palmer followed a few steps behind, flexing his fist around the axe handle.

He hugged the wall of the barn, working his way closer to the door where Bill Mitchell stood flattened against the planks with the Colt held ready. From beyond the corral a small object went arcing through the smoke towards the rear. It seemed to be catching the sun, though the sky was invisible under the grey pall.

'Dynamite,' Mitchell said laconically.

Palmer flinched and ducked as the explosion ripped through the back wall of the barn, but his father was already moving, heading in through the open door, the Colt spitting flame. Palmer took a fresh grip on the axe handle and followed, jumping over a body as he ran. Bullets ripped down from the loading-hatch above. Mitchell fired twice. A man plunged to the floor and lay still.

A sudden burst of fire came from the shadowy stalls on their left. Mitchell hit the dirt and Palmer hurled himself over the dividing wall, bringing the wooden handle down hard as he landed. The gunman squealed and the rifle dropped from his hand. He stared at Palmer, his unnaturally pale eye shining in the gloom. It was Whitey. Palmer grinned, remembering how the man had once offered to kill Bill Mitchell.

'Glad I never took you up on that,' he told the baffled cowhand as he brought the axe handle swinging across to lay him out cold.

He ducked warily from the stall, but there was nothing left to do. The explosion had flattened the far corner of the barn. One man lay dead, his chest ripped messily open by the blast, while another was struggling helplessly beneath a heap of splintered timber, both his legs broken. Red Corder leant against the wall with his head in his hands, blood streaming between his fingers to turn the faded russet hair to crimson. For the moment it looked like he was out of the fight.

Palmer made a move towards his father who was getting slowly to his knees.

'You all right?'

'Reckon so . . . Behind you, Billy!'

He whirled around. A figure had materialized out of the murk.

'Isn't that touching. The prodigal son returns home.' Slim Ketteridge stood in the doorway wreathed in smoke, the ranch house an inferno behind him, a rifle aimed steadily at Palmer's heart.

'If we're getting biblical I'm looking at the devil outa hell,' Bill Mitchell said, coming upright with the Peacemaker held ready.

'Oh no, that's where you're heading, not me.' Ketteridge cocked the rifle and moved closer to Palmer. 'Put down the Colt or I kill your son. You let me walk out of here and nobody else gets hurt.'

'No, Pop, don't do it,' Palmer said flatly, turning his back on Ketteridge. 'He won't keep his word, you know it.'

'Maybe I'd best count to three,' Ketteridge said. 'One . . .'

'Got no choice Billy.' Bill Mitchell let the Colt drop from his hand. 'I thought I'd killed you once, I can't risk losing you again. Go ahead, Slim, get going. Nobody's gonna stop you.'

'Especially you.' So fast Palmer could do nothing to stop him, Ketteridge stepped around him and fired, the Remington's bark deafening as the bullet zipped past his head.

With a feral scream of rage Palmer hurled himself at Ketteridge, knocking the rifle aside as it spat death for the second time. With all the power of his broad shoulders he heaved the gun from the other man's hands and flung it towards the fiery ruin of the ranch house.

Ketteridge reached for the six-gun at his side but Palmer's left hand was faster. He grabbed Ketteridge's fingers in his fist and squeezed, all the hatred within him finding an outlet in this act of vengeance. A red haze blurred his eyes. He'd come back to Serenity to see a lawman die, not knowing it was the wrong one, but he was about to put that right.

Ducking to dodge a wild punch from Ketteridge's other hand Palmer increased the pressure, relentlessly closing his fist like a vice and bringing his arm down to force the man to his knees, feeling bones break in his grasp. Blood oozed out between his fingers. Ketteridge squirmed, reaching blindly for the six-gun left-handed, only to have Palmer's right fist hammered on to his shoulder, exploding the joint apart.

Palmer was blind and deaf, seeing nothing but the body of his father as it fell to the dirt with a deadly red blossom flowering across his chest. Beneath him Ketteridge's face twisted in agony, mouth open to beg for mercy, but his words went unheard.

A hand gripped Palmer's arm and somebody reached past him to lift the gun from Ketteridge's holster.

'Enough, boy.'

He flipped round angrily, crimson fury still coursing through his veins, and came face to face with Quentin Jefferson. The old rancher was sombre, a deep sadness in his eyes.

'Your father would have wanted him to die according to the law. It's the least we can do.'

Gradually the tension eased from him. Palmer drew back his bandaged right hand and landed a haymaker on Ketteridge's chin. The man's eyes rolled up in his head and he fell senseless to the ground. Palmer got stiffly to his feet and looked around. All was quiet but for the merry crackle of fire as it raged through the ranch buildings. Red Corder's body had dropped across the splintered timbers, lit by a lurid glow. His boots pointed theatrically at the roof.

'Slim's second shot got him,' Quentin said. 'The last of Red's hired killers lit out. Buck an' the boys are rounding up the rest of his ranch hands.'

Palmer took a dozen faltering steps. Bill Mitchell lay staring at the swirling smoke, ash beginning to settle on his sightless eyes. His son knelt at his side and took hold of his hand.

'I'm sorry, Pa. I never got to tell you . . . ' Tears furrowed the dust on his cheeks. He was six years too late.

★ ★ ★

Serenity was full, the streets crowded with wagons and horses, men dodging the traffic as they crossed Main Street and headed for the gallows where the hangman and a couple of deputies stood waiting. Jake Jefferson sat in a wagon beside his father. He was even thinner than before and deathly pale, but he smiled as he looked down at the posy of flowers at his side and thought about his plans for the afternoon; Daisy had given up flirting to nurse him, her brief interest in Rufe Corder buried out in the foothills.

There was a festive air about the town; it wasn't every day a lawman got himself strung up. When the bell in the church tower struck the first chime of noon the door of the sheriff's office opened. The sheriff of Douglas County stepped out, a wide-brimmed hat on his head and a star pinned on his vest. Behind him, between two well-armed deputies, came the condemned man, his right hand heavily bandaged.

A dude in a brown suit pushed his way through the crowd, ignoring the jeers and jibes from the cowboys as he passed. He thrust himself in front of the sheriff, notebook and pencil held ready. 'You got anything to say to the readers of the *Eastern Gazette*, Sheriff?'

'Yes.' The lawman turned, the scar on his cheek pulling his mouth into a slight sardonic smile. 'Tell them justice is being done here today, though it took a little time. And make sure you get my name right. It's Mitchell. Billy Mitchell.'